The Complete Guide to books 1 to 4 from the 'Words from Daddy's Mouth' series

www.wordsfromdaddysmouth.com.au

ISBN: 978-0-9922716-8-8

www.wordsfromdaddysmouth.com.au

Published by D & M Fancy Pastry Pty Ltd

National Library of Australia Cataloguing-in-Publication entry:

Creator:	Burgess, Lily, author.
Title:	The complete guide to books one to four from the 'Words from Daddy's mouth' series / Lily Burgess; illustrated by Kate Hawthorne.
ISBN:	9780992271688 (paperback)
Series:	Burgess, Lily. Words from Daddy's mouth.
Target Audience:	For primary school age.
Subjects:	Reading (Primary) Reading--Parent participation Reading--Direct instruction approach.

Other Authors/Contributors: Hawthorne, Kate, illustrator.

Dewey Number: A823.4

CONTENTS

Book Four – The Brandings Game

ABOUT THE AUTHOR

About how this all began (and why Lily Burgess is the author on the cover of the books)

By Matthew Burgess

Being a full time lawyer I needed a creative outlet, and in 2010, began writing business books for other professional service providers.

However there was still something missing. My wife said she married me because I made her laugh with the crazy stories I told her when we first met and that I should write a book.

Many years later we began to raise 1, then 2, then 3 and finally 4, precious girls and I started to share stories of my childhood with them.

It soon became one of our family's favourite pastimes listening to these stories about my childhood. Often embellished and seldom kept on track the girls would be absorbed. What was fact became blurred in the magic of the stories told.

A strong undertone in the stories are various life lessons, while also ensuring a healthy dose of humour and role playing.

When my third daughter, Lily, was about four years old, she said "Daddy, please tell me another story from your mouth".

From that day on, the stories became known as "Words from Daddy's mouth". It was therefore a natural progression that Lily Burgess would became the pseudonym for the authoring of my children books to help distinguish them from my other publications.

With so many stories, we had to create a list to remember them all (at last count the list was nearing 500). So over time a game developed where the girls would choose a number from the list. Whatever story related to the number chosen would be the story that I would tell.

Stories were usually told as the last part of the wind down of an evening, sitting together in a bedroom or on a lounge chair.

ABOUT THE ILLUSTRATOR

From a young age, Kate Hawthorne aspired to write an amazing bio. But alas, this dream had to wait until she graduated from Miami University with two bachelors degrees in Fine Arts and Arts and Sciences. As a paper cut survivor she has created art for a wide variety of mediums from graphic novels, children's books, contests, costumes, theatre scenery, posters, newspapers, and even people's faces. She loves long walks through the art store, caffeinated beverages after midnight, and making everyone she meets laugh until they have sustained internal bleeding. Ask sometime to see her collection of rocks that look suspiciously unlike Bono.

On the following page are my steps for illustrating the *Big Rusty Nail* and all of the books in this series. Most illustrators and graphic novelists employ similar steps. However, different illustrators may make different choices at each step based on the style they are trying to achieve for their unique story, or they may even add different steps or take away steps. Art is ever evolving and a very diverse medium where so many dreams can be achieved.

1. First, I read the entire story through to see what I'm drawing and what the overall story and progression of the pictures should be.

2. Then I divide up the story into chunks of text. What I look for, when doing this, is sections that stay on a similar topic so that the story is broken up in a logical way. This also enables me to be able to draw an appropriate unique picture for a logical chunk of text.

3. Next I sketch the pages in pencil so that I can easily fix or change anything if necessary. I work with proportion, references to the style being used, and try to achieve a loose organic picture that will be the foundation for the rest of the steps.

4. After that I slowly and precisely ink the pages with India ink, which is permanent, waterproof, and very dark. Inking is an important step as it cleans up the lines, creates lines that my scanner is able to better pick up, and tightens and focuses all the details. An inked drawing is also easier to colour in once this becomes a digital document, as with pencil there are rouge pixels.

5. This next step has a lot of mini-steps that include scanning the pages, several steps that convert them into a smooth digital copy, making the lines darker, getting rid of rouge pixels, cleaning the lines, preparing layers, and then the last part of this step is to lay in flat colours all over the document.

6. Next I shade everything by hand from the smallest details to the largest objects so that I can achieve the shading for the exact area I need. There are many different

techniques for shading but the approach I take is to make the illustrations look very young, bright, and cartoony.

7. The final step is to add line shading, black lines/tic marks along where the shading goes. This specific shading detail for this style adds extra character and design and makes the drawings seem more complete. I also do detail work on this step such as putting the entire cross hatching on the school kids hats or filling in lines that got erased or covered during all the previous steps.

Portfolio: http://katejellyfish.weebly.com/

NOTES

Paperback page references are shown in italics for easy referencing.

Referencing in this book refers to pages within this guide.

– the –
Big Rusty Nail

by Lily Burgess
Illustrated by Kate Hawthorne

The Big Rusty Nail

This is a work of fiction. Any similarity to persons living or dead is merely coincidental.

This book is licensed for your personal use only. If in electronic format a separate copy of this book should be purchased for each person for whom this book is shared. Neither the author nor publisher assumes a duty of care in connection this book. Some or all of the material in this book may be fictional and for legal purposes you should treat this book as entertainment only and not for instruction.

Book One
The Big Rusty Nail

By Lily Burgess

"Do you remember how I had to repeat Year 6 because I broke my right arm?" asked Dad.

Jaz and Stephanie nodded, recalling the story.

"Actually I broke my left arm too. I broke my right arm first. Then a few weeks after it had healed, I broke my left arm.

"So, for about six months all I could do at school was play 'Lemonade Stand' on the computer. Back then, our school only had one computer—it was an Apple II.

"Can you believe it? One computer for the whole school— just one for six hundred kids!"

Dad put his right arm in front of him, miming a broken arm, and then pretended to press keys on an imaginary keyboard with his left fingers. Then he changed his mime to his left arm being broken and tapped on the imaginary keyboard with his right hand.

Jaz giggled, and Dad finished his mime act.

"Now these days, you call your computer a 'Mac,'" Dad said. "Our school computer was a very early version of a Mac—an Apple Macintosh II."

Dad paused, thinking. "Year 6 is the last year of Primary School. Being the oldest kids in the school, our year level had special responsibilities. Guess what I was responsible for?" Dad paused again, but Stephanie and Jaz remained silent, waiting to hear what Dad would say.

SIMPSON

"Actually, come to think of it," Dad went on, "I was responsible for four things!

"First, I was captain of one of the sports teams. Our team was called Simpson, and our team colour was red. I made a huge flag out of a triangular piece of bright red material. I painted 'Simpson' on it in big, bold letters using white paint. Then I attached the flag to a long, wooden pole. (I think it might have been an old broom handle.)

"I would take it to sports carnivals and wave it like this."

Dad stood up and waved his arms back and forth, while swaying his whole body, demonstrating how he used to hold the flag.

"That was my first responsibility. My second was to be a library monitor. I checked that everyone brought their books back to the library.

"This was a great job, especially when I got to miss some lessons." Mum shook her head.

"My third responsibility was to be the captain of the school soccer team. I was a pretty good soccer player although that is a story for another day." Dad quickly glanced at Mum, who was rolling her eyes.

Dad continued.

"Soccer was my favourite sport, but I also participated in cross-country running, cricket, softball, British bulldogs 1, 2, 3, and brandings." Mum rolled her eyes again.

"Okay, British bulldogs 1, 2, 3 and brandings are not really sports, but they were lots of fun.

"Come to think of it, brandings was not something I was particularly good at, given that I broke my left arm while playing it. That reminds me of another story that also happened that year, the day I had to play soccer in my red undies! But that is a story for another day.

"Finally, my fourth responsibility (and this is what this story is about) was to be a sports room monitor. Do you know what a sports room monitor does?"

Jaz and Stephanie shrugged their shoulders.

"A sports monitor runs the whole sports room!" Dad announced proudly.

"Can you believe it?

"Our sports room was about the size of the storeroom next to your hall at school—about three metres by four metres."

Dad stood up and paced out the size of the sports room, then returned to his seat.

"This room with all the sports equipment was run by the students. When a student wanted to borrow something, we would write down all the details in a book: the date and time, the person's name and class they were in, and the equipment they borrowed. It was a super fun job."

"Steph and Jaz, can you guess what sort of equipment we had?"

Jaz and Stephanie shrugged their shoulders again.

"There were cricket balls, bats, and stumps. Baseball bats, gloves, and balls. We had soccer balls, footballs, tennis balls, and handballs. However, some of the best items were these really bouncy balls. They were very popular."

"Like mine?" Stephanie asked.

"Very similar, Steph. The balls were about the same size as your miniature netball," Dad said. "But they were made out of a really rubbery, very bouncy material. From memory, they were bright blue or red.

"The kids loved them because you could throw them very far and kick them really, really hard."

"That reminds me. We used to play a game where everyone had to stand in a circle with one person on the outside with a bouncy ball. Then we took turns to throw the ball into the circle. The aim was to try and hit someone. When someone was hit, they had to stand outside the circle."

"Fun!" said Jaz.

"It was such fun," mused Dad, "but back to the story.

"Ooh, I forgot we had other equipment too. Skipping ropes, small ones and really big ones. Medicine balls, which are balls that are very, very heavy. Even a parachute—a real parachute! It was really great equipment."

"What about hula hoops?" asked Jaz.

"Yes! I forgot about them too!" Dad smiled. "So we had all of those things in the sports room."

Then Dad remembered something else, and he added, "We also had one of those big mattresses for landing on when you do high jump. It was a gigantic mattress, and it needed about twenty kids to drag it around.

Jaz and Stephanie looked bewildered by this.

So Dad tried again and said, "Imagine, twenty little kids pushing a mattress about the size of a rubbish truck!" Jaz, Stephanie, and Mum all cracked up with laughter at the thought. "Okay, back to the story," Dad continued.

"There would be at least two of us in the equipment room, sometimes three.

"The school rule was that kids were not allowed to go to the sports room to borrow the equipment until ten minutes after the first lunch bell had rung. This meant the kids only had about half an hour to borrow and use the equipment."

"That is not a lot of time," said Jaz.

"No, it is not."

"What would happen, Jaz," Dad continued, "is when we opened up the door to the sports room, there would be a very long queue. Kids would be lined up as far as we could see.

"Everyone would be shouting, 'What about me? Pick me, pick me! What's going on? I really want to get my stuff!

Help me, help me!' So there was a big rush to get the equipment out of the sports room.

"That is why we took turns writing up the information in the exercise book and running around the sports room finding the equipment. It was very tiring."

"Which job did you like doing most?" Stephanie asked.

"I liked taking the names," stated Dad, "and you will soon find out why." He grinned at Mum.

"You see, there was something rather odd beside the big mattress. I am still not sure exactly what it was. It was a big, triangular piece of wood, and it had lots of wooden spikes coming out of it that were about twenty centimetres long—but the whole thing was falling apart. It was taller than me."

Stephanie stood up. "This tall?" she demonstrated, stretching her arms up as high as she could.

"Yes," agreed Dad, "about two metres high." He paused for a moment.

"Now that I think about it, it was probably intended to hang up quoits and similar stuff like hula hoops. That is most likely why it had spikes poking out of it, to hang stuff on.

"Back when I was a kid, I did not understand what it was about because we did not use it. It just sat right in the middle of the equipment room, wedged against the mattress, with no obvious purpose."

"Do you remember what I told you about how the equipment went out of the room?"

Stephanie and Jaz both shouted, "In a big rush."

"Well, when it came back in, it was in an even bigger rush. We would try and put it all away quickly so we also had some time to play before the end of lunch.

"Actually, even if we were running late, we would play around after the lunch bell had rung. Then, when we were late for class, we would say to the teachers, 'I'm a sports monitor,' and they would assume it must have been a busy lunch time. Best of all, we did not get into trouble. It was a pretty cool gig."

Stephanie and Jaz looked at each other and giggled, while Mum grimaced.

"To tidy up, we had to put all the equipment back where it belonged.

"Remember those bouncy balls I talked about earlier? They had to be returned to some shelving right up near the roof. Unfortunately, the shelf was too high for us to reach, so instead we would throw the balls and try to get them to land on the shelves.

"Looking back on it, this was not a very good idea—especially as they would bounce all over the place. If you threw a ball really hard, it would bounce about and hit another kid. Sometimes on their head!

"Really it was quite dangerous.

"Although sometimes it was fun when it would bounce near the mattress. We could do a superman dive onto the mattress and shout, 'Yes, wotta catch!'" Again Mum grimaced.

"Now, on this particular day when we opened the sports room, we discovered that the monitors from the previous day had not finished tidying up.

"The room was a mess. There was equipment all over the place. In particular, those bouncy balls were everywhere, including one that was stuck between the mattress and the big wooden thing with the spikes.

"That day everyone wanted a bouncy ball, and before long we had lent out all the balls—except for the one that was stuck.

"Then a kid comes along who really wants one of those balls.

"He became very cranky and threatened to dob on us to the teachers for not getting him a ball."

"This day it was my job to collect the equipment. The other sports monitors shouted, 'Hey Matt (that is me), get that ball out,' pointing to the ball that was stuck.

"We were already late, so I rushed over and I looked down between the mattress and the big wooden thing. I could see where the ball was stuck, so I put my arm straight down like this."

Dad stood up to demonstrate. Then he bent over and put his arm straight down as if reaching into a tight spot.

"I grabbed the ball, but at the same time something scratched my arm."

"One of the wooden spikes!" screamed Jaz.

"Worse," winced Dad. "It was a big nail, a big rusty nail."

Mum shuddered, while Stephanie and Jaz gasped.

"But there is more," Dad continued.

"It was quite gloomy in the equipment room and because I was going down arm first into the gap, I could not see the nail sticking out. Next thing I knew, I could feel something digging into my arm. I thought, 'Ooh, what is that?' Then my arm started to hurt—a lot.

"I moved a little and saw the rusty nail in the big wooden thing sticking into my arm. The nail was so rusty—it reminds me of how rusty my car floor was. So rusty that my foot hit the ground when I tried to put on the brake!"

"Wooh!" said Jaz.

"Anyway, back to the story. The big rusty nail was stuck deep into my arm and I started to try and pull my arm out, but there was a bigger problem about to happen. I pulled my arm up at the wrong angle! The next thing I knew, the nail started going in even deeper!

"Do you know what I felt then?"

Stephanie and Jaz froze.

"I felt the nail hit the bone in my arm!" Dad said, looking slightly pale, while Mum giggled.

"Whoa!" shrieked Jaz.

"Then I started screaming. My arm hurt so much.

"Actually, the scar is still on my arm."

Dad showed his arm to Jaz and Stephanie. "Can you see that, girls?" he asked.

"Yes," said Jaz.

"It is tiny now," Dad explained. "But you can see that white line on my arm. That is the scar."

Steph and Jaz were starting to look pale as well, so Dad got back to the story.

"Do you know what happened when I pulled my arm out? Do you know what I could see?"

"The bone?" gasped Stephanie.

"Yes," said Dad. "The bone AND the flesh inside my arm— just this white stuff. It was totally white." Dad paled further as he remembered what the bone looked like, while Mum chuckled.

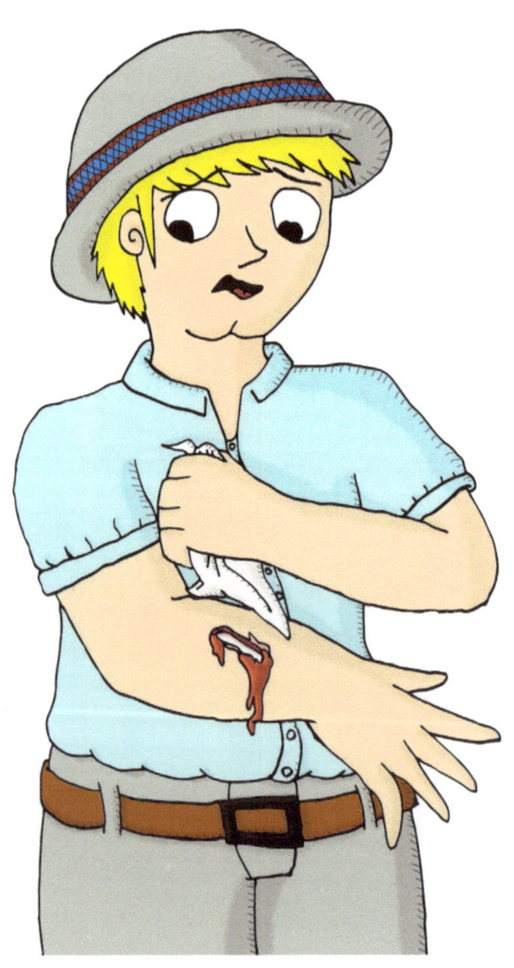

"Ewwwww," shuddered Stephanie.

"Then something else started to happen!" Dad was now turning green, while Mum continued to giggle.

Stephanie and Jasmin were speechless. Dad bravely continued.

"Suddenly, the white flesh turned into the brightest red blood—about the same colour as the Simpson flag.

"Then blood started pouring out. There was a lot of blood. It was gushing out everywhere.

"Oohhh! I can still feel the pain now." Dad shivered.

"I quickly gathered some tissues from my pocket and pushed them into the hole in my arm. I was in so much pain, but I refused to cry.

"I could hear my friends saying, 'Hey Matt, what's wrong? Hurry up and get that ball! What are you doing?'

"I went over and showed them my arm. I said, 'Look at this, look at my arm.' 'Ewww,' they said and then, 'Oh my goodness!'

"Do you know what they then said to me? Well, the boy who wanted the ball said, 'You'd better not tell anyone.' Can you believe it! All I could think was that I was going to have to tell someone. It hurt a lot and I was in danger with that deep cut and blood going everywhere.

"Plus, someone else might get hurt on the big wooden thing. It would be irresponsible not to tell someone at least about the rusty nail.

"My friends and I patched my arm up as best as we could with an old clean cloth we found in a cupboard. We did not tell the teachers about what had happened to me because we hoped the bleeding would stop at some stage.

"However, we did tell the PE—'PE' stands for 'Physical Education'—teacher that we had, by chance, noticed that there were some big rusty nails sticking out of the big wooden thing in the sports room.

"Do you know what the teacher said? He said he did not know why the school had that wooden thing, or why it was in the sports room! 'It is always getting in the way,' he said. 'We should throw it out!'

"So they did. The school threw out the big wooden thing with the wooden spikes and big rusty nails. Can you believe it! So it did not hurt anyone, ever again.

"And, although the sore on my arm was there for a very long time, it did eventually heal and just left the scar as a reminder."

"Ewwwww," said Stephanie and Jaz in unison.

The Big Rusty Nail is an entertaining journey of a day in the life of a primary school sports room monitor, shared between a dad and his young children.

The story also provides a modern take on the proverb 'A Stitch in Time Saves Nine'. That is, stopping something before it happens is often better than having to fix things up after the event.

www.wordsfromdaddysmouth.com.au

$14.95
ISBN 978-0-9873910-9-4

Teacher's
guide

the big
rusty nail

The Big Rusty Nail

By Lily Burgess

Illustrated by Kate Hawthorne

ISBN: 978-0-9873910-9-4 (paperback)

ISBN: 978-0-9873910-7-0 (ebook)

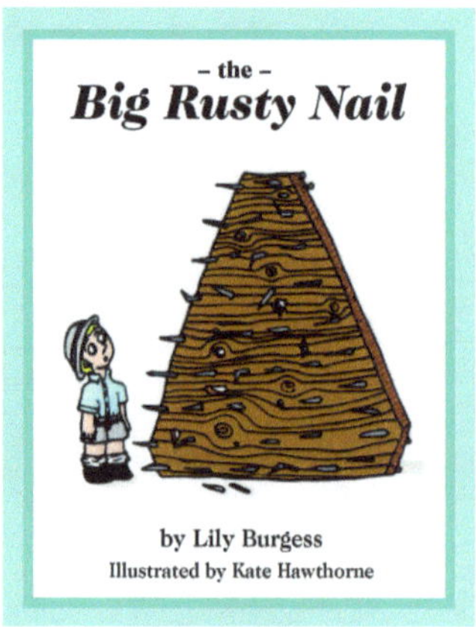

Teachers' Notes

Prepared and written by a teacher with experience in both whole class and special education

These notes are made available free of charge for use in schools.

They may not be reproduced and sold commercially without prior permission of publisher.

Please email contact@wordsfromdaddysmouth.com.au for further information

The Big Rusty Nail

1 Synopsis

The Big Rusty Nail is a tale about a young boy who accidentally stabbed his arm on a rusty nail, while attempting to retrieve a misplaced ball in the school sports room. Although the wound is serious, the other students try to convince him not to tell the teachers.

2 Background

This story (although somewhat embellished) is based on an actual event. It took place in the 1980s, in the Australian Capital Territory. It is one in a series of stories. Luckily, this story has a happy ending, and the wound healed without medical intervention. However, the consequences of not seeking medical help could have been dire.

3 Themes

Reminiscing about childhood experiences:

- Student responsibilities;
- Standing up to peer pressure;
- Making decisions about appropriate and inappropriate behaviours; and
- The need to tell adults when a mishap occurs.

4 Writing style

This story is written in the conversational style of a father recounting a childhood event to his daughters, as told through the voice his daughter, Lily.

As the text involves some narration and considerable dialogue, the tenses vary accordingly.

Direct speech is marked by quotation marks (inverted commas). Where there is extended direct speech, continuing over more than one paragraph, the text follows the convention of beginning each paragraph with quotation marks, but only using closing quotation marks at the conclusion of a section of dialogue.

The story also includes a series of digressions, as the father explains concepts and interacts with his daughters.

5 Study notes

To introduce the story:

a Ask the students if their parents/ grandparents have ever told stories about their childhood.

- Explain that this is a story a father tells to his daughters.

- Read the introductory notes on Page v (*paperback p. 4*).

- Show students the front cover, read the title, ask them to predict what a story about rusty nail might entail, and what the pictured brown triangular object might be.

- Ask students what they know about rusty nails (What would make a nail go rusty? What would happen if they cut themselves on a rusty nail?…)
- Read the story for enjoyment.

Following the reading of the story:

- Discuss the two layers to the story (Dad telling a story to his daughters, and the story about the rusty nail). Discuss this with reference to the illustration on Page 12 (*paperback p. 12*).
- Identify the main characters in each layer (Dad, his daughters Stephanie, Jaz and Mum in the first layer, and Dad as a young boy, his school friends and teachers in the second layer).
- Ask the students to draw two pictures – one depicting the family listening to Dad telling the story, and the other, showing Dad as a young boy, injuring himself on a rusty nail.
- Create a story line for the rusty nail story.
- Identify the digressions (early computers, responsibilities in the final year of Primary school, sports and games, the rusty car floor…).
- Discuss how the digressions help to provide context and background to the main story.

6 Activities

- Ask students to record or video a parent or grandparent re-telling a story from their childhood.

- Invite a parent or grandparent to the school to retell a childhood experience (Grandparent Day activity).

- Discuss whether or not the students were responsible in deciding not to tell the teacher about the wound.

- Discuss whether the alternative the students chose (reporting a dangerous piece of equipment) was a responsible decision.

7 Drama

Role-play alternative endings, using hypotheticals such as:

a The students tell the teachers about the injured arm, and they arrange appropriate medical attention.

- The wound becomes infected, and the student has to go to hospital.

8 Mathematics

a Measurement – various sizes, heights and lengths are mentioned (the size of the sports room [p. 9], (*paperback p. 11*), the height of the triangular piece of wood [p. 16], (*paperback p. 18*), and the size of the wooden spikes [p. 16] (*paperback p. 18*)). Measure/pace these out in the playground.

b Do a stock-take of the school sports room equipment.

- Graph the number of balls, skipping ropes, hoops etc.

- Consider what new pieces of equipment the school might need.

9 Writing

Make a wish list of new items for the school sports room.

- Write a persuasive argument for these items; and

- Make diary entries describing the events that took place in the story

10 Health

- Discuss wound care, the consequences of a wound becoming infected, and the need for anti-tetanus injections.

11 Science

- Rust (or oxidation) occurs when iron comes into contact with moisture and air. Carry out experiments to investigate how and why an iron nail becomes rusty.

- For some suggested experiments see:

  http://www.msm.cam.ac.uk/SeeK/rustynails.htm
  http://www.nuffieldfoundation.org/practical-chemistry/causes-rusting
  http://www.terrificscience.org/lessonpdfs/nailingrust.pdf

12 Worksheets

- Comprehension
- Word Study
- Crossword
- Word Search

The Big Rusty Nail

Comprehension Sheet

Who is listening to Dad's story telling?

____

____

What were Dad's four responsibilities when he was in his last year of Primary School?

`1` ____

`2` ____

`3` ____

`4` ____

List ten items in the school sports room.

____

____

____

Describe what happened when the big rusty nail stabbed Dad's arm?

What would you do if a big rusty nail stabbed your arm?

What might have happened if Dad's wound had become infected?

What would you do if another student told you not to tell the teacher when you were injured?

The Big Rusty Nail.

Word study. Write down meanings for these words.

responsible

speechless

demonstrate

explain

remember

giggle

bouncy

'Monitor' has several meanings. Draw a picture for each meaning.

Computer monitor	School monitor	Monitor lizard

Look at this word

nail

Break it into two sounds

n – ail

Now complete this table

Read words	Sound	Re - write word	Draw a picture
nail	n – ail		
sail	s – ail		
pail	p – ail		
tail	t – ail		
hail	h – ail		
jail	j – ail		
mail	m – ail		
quail	qu – ail		
rail	r – ail		

This story mentions several colours. Sometimes colours are used to describe a face – and tell us how that person feels.

Read words	Explain feelings	Draw pictures
red face		
white face		
green face		
blue face		

Word building – read and write these words

rust	rusts	rusty	rusted	rusting

The Big Rusty Nail

Across

2. Dad has a ________ on his arm.

4. 'Lemonade Stand' was a ________ game.

5. How many computers were at Dad's school?

6. Dad scratched his arm on a ________ nail.

7. The bouncy balls were red and ________.

8. How many kids did it take to move the mattress?

Down

1. What was Dad's favourite sport?

2. What was the name of Dad's sports team?

3. The nail hit the ________ in Dad's arm.

The Big Rusty Nail

```
z p f u l s h v e h e e c e b
e v s x r w b n n u q x h h a
s s t s n n j e h l u e l y l
i o u o e o j r f a i r u v l
y c m f t o t o t h p c m m m
b c p t b j g p d o m i z u a
e e s b a v u e b o e s h e t
i r l a l y d h z p n e f v t
i o u l l x n y l s t d d x r
w t d l p a r a c h u t e q e
c r i c k e t n t k l v q u s
c r o s s c o u n t r y i o s
d o x h a n d b a l l u q i k
s k i p p i n g x n x j z t r
b a t s p o r t s d e l h l b
```

ball	bat	cricket
crosscountry	equipment	exercise
handball	hulahoops	mattress
netball	parachute	quoit
rope	skipping	soccer
softball	sports	stumps

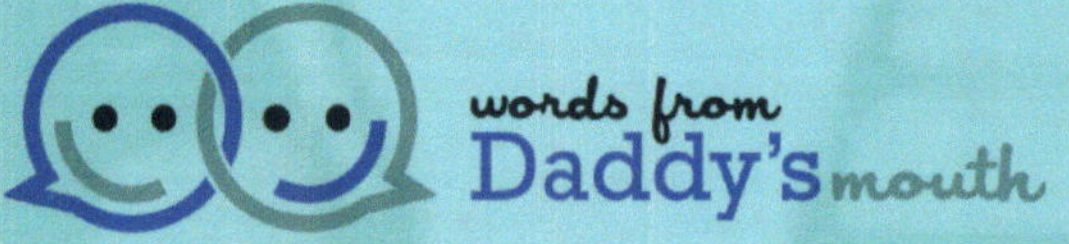

– the –
Terrible Red Racer

by Lily Burgess

Illustrated by Kate Hawthorne

The Terrible Red Racer

This is a work of fiction. Any similarity to persons living or dead is merely coincidental.

This book is licensed for your personal use only. If in electronic format, a separate copy of this book should be purchased for each person for whom this book is shared. Neither the author nor publisher assumes a duty of care in connection with this book. Some or all of the material in this book may be fictional and for legal purposes you should treat this book as entertainment only and not for instruction.

www.wordsfromdaddysmouth.com.au

Published by D & M Fancy Pastry Pty Ltd

Book Two

The Terrible Red Racer

By Lily Burgess

"Girls, do you remember how I had to repeat Year 6?" asked Dad.

Jasmin and Stephanie both nodded.

Then Jasmin asked, "Is this 'The Big Rusty Nail' story?"

"No," said Dad, "this is the story about how I broke my arm."

"But Dad," said Stephanie, "didn't you break both your arms in Year 6?"

"At the same time?" screeched Jasmin.

"No," said Dad, "fortunately not at the same time. I broke my right arm, and then a few weeks after it healed and the plaster came off, I broke my left arm."

"Then all you did was play 'Lemonade Stand' on the Apple II computer!" laughed Stephanie.

"That is right, Stephanie. At school, all I did was play 'Lemonade Stand' for six months because I agreed to ride The Terrible Red Racer."

"The Terrible Red Racer!" Stephanie and Jasmin yelled in unison as Mum rolled her eyes.

Dad lowered his voice to a whisper. "Yes, The Terrible Red Racer."

"I did not know that you had a red racing bike, Dad," said Jasmin.

"I did not," said Dad then he lowered his voice. "That was part of the problem." Mum rolled her eyes again.

"You see, Jasmin, I lent my yellow BMX bike to one of my best friends in primary school, Jeremy Tobin.

"Jeremy and I used to play together all the time.

"We mainly used to play at his house because he had so many toys. He was the first person at our school to get a Commodore 64 computer."

"A what?" asked Jasmin.

"Were they cool?" interrupted Stephanie.

"A Commodore 64 was like an Xbox or Wii, Jasmin, and they were more than cool, Stephanie," said Dad. "At the time, they were totally awesome."

"Unfortunately, to load up a simple game like 'Ping,' it took about half an hour because the game was loaded onto the computer with a cassette tape."

"Dad, what is a cassette tape?" Jasmin asked.

"Yes, Matthew, explain that one," Mum giggled.

"Mmmmm," mused Dad. "Perhaps the kids can 'Google' it later."

"Get on with the story, Dad," said Stephanie.

"All right," said Dad. "On this particular day, near the beginning of the term for Year 6, we had a student free day. Do you girls know what that means?"

"Yes!" exclaimed Jasmin. "It means that the kids get to stay home while the teachers have to go to school!"

"Exactly," said Dad, "but on this particular day, our soccer teacher offered to have a practice session when we would normally have big lunch. I stayed at home all morning, and then around the middle of the day, I rode my BMX bike to Jeremy's house. That way we could ride to soccer practice together."

"When I got to Jeremy's house, he showed me the brand-new red racing bike he had been given for his birthday.

"It was a very big bike. So big that Jeremy needed to give me a boost up to get on it!

"It was the right size for Jeremy because he was taller than me, but for some reason, that to this day I am unsure of, Jeremy said that he really wanted to ride my yellow BMX bike. He asked me to ride his brand-new red racer.

"While the red racer looked much like any other bike, there was one part of it that was very different. It had a triangular-shaped, grey covered case that sat on the joint between the main frame of the bike and the handlebars, and it had three big red buttons on it, as well as a key."

"What was it for?" asked Stephanie.

"I asked the same thing of Jeremy," said Dad.

"Jeremy explained to me that it was a special new invention that allowed you to lock the bike without the need of a chain."

"How did that work exactly, Dad?" asked Jasmin.

"Not very well," frowned Dad, as Mum giggled in the background.

"Basically, what the invention was designed to do was to lock the handlebars in place so that they could not be moved in any direction, and, for reasons that you will hear about shortly, it was an idea that did not gain much popularity.

"Jeremy gave me a boost up onto the red racer, then he jumped onto my yellow BMX yelling, 'Bet I can beat you there, Burgo!' Then he raced off down the street."

"Jeremy had a fifty-metre lead before I got going. There were two ways to ride to school—on the bike track and through a tunnel, or on the road with the cars. By the time I got to the end of the street to turn onto the bicycle track, I could see Jeremy was already in the tunnel that went under the bridge near our school.

"I knew that the tunnel came out quite a long way away from where we were to meet for soccer. To have any chance at winning the race, I decided it would be quicker to cross the road in front of the school using the zebra crossing."

"Unfortunately, while the decision seemed smart at first, it soon proved to be wrong. As I came towards the zebra crossing, I saw a car coming down the street. Instead of going straight across the road, I needed to turn left and continue along the footpath to stay away from the approaching car."

Dad paled.

"Guess what happened when I tried to turn left?"

"I know," giggled Stephanie.

"What?" Jasmin asked, with a worried voice.

"The handlebars locked! OUTRAGEOUS!" Stephanie shouted then rolled about laughing.

"Thanks, Stephanie," said Dad. "The whizz-bang new invention of locking handlebars somehow locked without the key. So instead of the bike turning left, it continued going straight ahead. To make matters worse, there was a big bump on the path that caused me to ride straight over the gutter and onto the road at the exact time the car was approaching."

"At this stage, all I could think was that I had to try to get off the road before the car hit me. So I tried to jump off The Terrible Red Racer, but my leg got caught in the handlebars that were still locked tight. Then I fell very quickly towards the road.

"By now, the lady driving the car had seen me. She slammed her brakes so hard that the car made a screeching sound that was even louder than the horn that she started beeping.

"As I fell to the ground, my body twisted. I then thought I had better push myself off the road as quickly as possible, so I put my right arm straight out to give me something to push off from."

"Guess what happened when my hand hit the road?"

"What, Dad?" gasped Jasmin, looking concerned.

Dad paused for a minute and then stood up. Suddenly he clapped his hands very loudly and yelled, "SNAP!"

Jasmin and Stephanie both jumped.

"Snap?" squealed Jasmin.

"Yes," said Dad, paling further. "The bone in my right forearm snapped. It was like breaking a chopstick over your knee."

"Then I looked up. I was lying underneath the front of the car, which had come to a stop. I rolled out, and the lady was standing over me and screaming, 'Move that bike! Get off the road!'"

"I tried to stand up, but my right arm felt as though it weighed a thousand million kilograms. I gasped, 'I am moving as fast as I can. I think I have dislocated my shoulder.'

"The lady continued yelling at me, 'Move that bike! Get off the road!'"

"Dad, I thought you broke your arm," interrupted Stephanie.

"Yes, I did break my arm, but I did not realise it at first," said Dad. "I looked down at my arm and I noticed that the bone was sticking out at right angles. I then realised that I had probably not dislocated my shoulder. However, I was not entirely sure what had happened."

"The lady driving the car was still yelling at me as she drove off. While I was upset with her at the time, the reality was that I had been pretty irresponsible and had probably scared her more than I had scared myself.

"To this day, I still do not know how I managed to move Jeremy's Terrible Red Racer off the road. Somehow I dragged it all the way to the front door of the school office, which was about 150 metres away.

"There was no way I could ride the bike anymore. In fact, I could barely walk. I went to the front desk of the school and asked the lady at reception if I could phone my mum because I had hurt my arm."

"Why didn't you just use your iPhone, Dad?" asked Stephanie.

"Stephanie," said Dad, "there were no such things as mobile phones, let alone smartphones when I was at school. In fact, we had only one cassette player in our whole family for many, many years."

"Now that is really outrageous, please stop talking about cassettes and get on with the story, Dad," demanded Stephanie.

"Okay! The point was that unless I could convince the lady at the school to let me use the school's phone, there was no way I was going to be able to get in contact with my mum," Dad continued.

"The lady on reception looked at my arm. Then she looked at me and frowned and said, 'It is a student free day today and no students are allowed inside the school. Please leave.'

"Again, I showed the lady my arm and said, 'Please, I am in a lot of pain.' She then said, 'No students are allowed in the school. Leave the building immediately.'

"She held my left arm and marched me out of the office, and I went out onto the front lawn of the school. Then I lay down to save some energy and tried to think about what I could do next. After a little while, I decided that I needed to go back into the school and plead with the lady to allow me to make one quick phone call to my mum."

"While holding my arm, I slowly struggled to my feet. Just as I got to the front door, the lady jumped up from her desk, ran over, slammed the door shut, and then locked it so that I could not get in! Then she yelled through the window, 'Go away! You are not welcome! GO AWAY!'

"By now, I had lost all my energy. I collapsed on the front lawn of the school and just lay there, unable to move.

"I am still not sure how long I lay there, but at some stage later in the day, guess who came along?"

"Our mum," guessed Jasmin.

"Mum and Dad had not met yet, Jasmin," said Dad smiling.

"Who was it, Dad?" asked Jasmin.

"My mum," said Dad.

"Gran?" Stephanie asked with wide eyes.

"Yes, that is right, your gran," said Dad.

"What was she doing there?" asked Jasmin.

"That is a very good question, Jasmin," said Dad. "Apparently, I found out afterwards, one of the parents who lived across the road from the school saw me lying next to The Terrible Red Racer on the front lawn of the school. Noticing I had not moved for an extended period of time, they eventually rang my mum and said, 'Mrs Burgess, is your son meant to be lying on the front lawn of the school at the moment, not moving?'

"Gran apparently said, 'Oh, my goodness!'"

Mum started to giggle and then burst out laughing so hard she got tears in her eyes.

"Muuum, you are ruining the story," Jasmin said.

"Sorry," Mum said muffling her laughter.

"Okay, where were we?" Dad asked, getting the story back on track. "Yes, Gran got the phone call. Based on that call, Gran got in the car and drove to school to see if I was actually lying down on the grass.

"As soon as Gran saw my arm, she knew immediately that it had been broken as she had worked in an X-ray department and had seen lots of broken bones. She took me straight to the hospital that was closest to the school."

"Unfortunately, that was when things started to go wrong," said Dad.

"How could things have become any worse, Dad?" asked Stephanie as Mum wiped her eyes, still giggling.

"Well," said Dad, now beginning to shake a little and wince at the thought of the next part of the story. Jasmin and Stephanie moved closer.

"Matthew, finish the story please," said Mum, stifling her giggles.

"Okay," said Dad waking himself up from his daydream. "Sorry. Where were we up to?"

"You had just arrived at the hospital," said Stephanie.

"That is right," said Dad. "I was checked into the emergency section of the hospital. We waited there for around forty minutes, and eventually one of the doctors came along and asked, 'Why are you here?'

"I showed the doctor my arm. He took my mum and I into a treatment room. Then he said, 'That needs an X-ray. However, clearly the bone has been broken.' Then he gave me a needle to numb the area to have it ready to be pulled back into place.

"The doctor asked my mum and me to go back to the emergency waiting area. We sat there for around two hours."

"During this time, I lost count of how many other people were helped. In fact, many of the people who were helped had arrived after us.

"Eventually, Gran went and asked one of the nurses when it would be my turn. Within a few minutes, another doctor came along and looked at my arm.

"We explained that the earlier doctor had confirmed that my arm would need to be pulled back into place and that I had been given a needle. The second doctor nodded and agreed with this. Then he took me into another treatment room."

"Guess what happened then?" asked Dad.

"What?" asked Jasmin as her eyes widened.

"The doctor asked a nurse to hold one end of my arm like this, while the doctor held my hand and wrist."

Dad stood up and asked Jasmin to hold his hand while Stephanie held the top of his arm.

"Now," said Dad, "on the count of three, each of you pull in the opposite direction as hard as you can.

"One, two, three, PULL!" yelled Dad.

Just as Stephanie and Jasmin pulled his arm, Dad screamed loudly, "ARRRGGHHHH!" Stephanie and Jasmin fell to the ground laughing.

"Guess why I screamed?" asked Dad.

"Because it hurt a lot," said Stephanie.

"Yes," said Dad, "but it was not a normal kind of hurt. What we found out later was that the needle that I had been given numbed my arm for only thirty minutes."

"But they had given you the needle over two hours earlier!" said Stephanie, remembering the story.

"Exactly!" yelled Dad. "This meant that there was nothing numbing my arm at all." Dad turned green at the thought. Mum giggled.

"Once the doctor had found this out, he said, 'Why didn't you say so earlier! You will need to go to the big hospital at the other end of town where they give you a needle that puts you to sleep. Then they will fix your arm up.'"

"It was now almost night-time and Gran said, 'You will have to go to the hospital by yourself. I need to go home to look after your sister and brother. I also need to help your dad as he is so sick he cannot get out of bed, and the builders have been working on the renovations today and sanded back the kitchen. Apparently, there is an inch of dust in the kitchen plus I have not even eaten today. Oh, my goodness! What a mess this is.'"

"Outrageous!" squealed Stephanie and Dad nodded in agreement.

"Because Gran had to leave, it was agreed that there was only one way to get me to the hospital. Can you guess what that was?"

"How, Dad?" asked Jasmin with a bright spark in her eyes.

"Well," said Dad, "how do people get to a hospital in an emergency?"

"In an ambulance!" screeched Stephanie.

"An ambulance?" asked Jasmin, giggling.

"Yes, an ambulance!" exclaimed Dad.

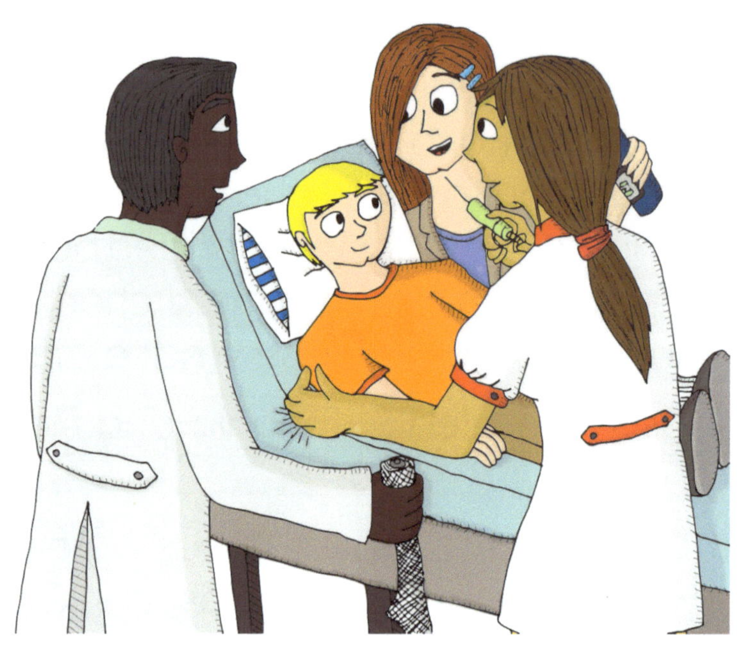

"A real ambulance?" asked Jasmin with wide eyes.

"Yes, Jasmin, a real ambulance," said Dad, smiling.

"By the time I was put in the ambulance, it was night-time and the medical staff really looked after me," continued Dad.

"When I got to the big hospital, the doctor and nurses there also looked after me really well. They explained exactly what was going to happen.

"They talked me through how I would go to sleep after they gave me two more needles. Then while I was asleep, the doctor and nurses would put the bones in my arm back in place.

"Once the bones were back in place, a big plaster cast would go over my hand, all the way up my forearm, over my elbow, and finish halfway up the top of my arm like this."

Dad held his arm out in front of him with his elbow bent at a right angle to show exactly how his arm was going to look after everything had happened.

"And guess what?" asked Dad.

"What?" responded Jasmin, jumping slightly.

"Everything that the doctor and nurses, told me was going to happen, happened exactly as they promised, but there was one little thing that they forgot to mention. I remember to this day the event that was the worst part of all of the events that day."

"Worse than actually breaking your arm, Dad?" asked Stephanie.

"Yes," said Dad in a lowered voice.

"Worse than the handlebars locking on The Terrible Red Racer?" asked Jasmin.

"Yes," said Dad, lowering his voice further and moving closer to Jasmin and Stephanie.

"Worse than having your arm pulled back into shape without any anaesthetic?" asked Mum.

"Yes," said Dad, again lowering his voice and creeping closer.

"What was it?" spluttered Stephanie, beginning to tremble.

Dad paused again, increasing the tension, then whispered, "Guess where they put the last needle before I went to sleep—and before I tell you, keep in mind that it was this big."

Dad held his hands about thirty centimetres apart and paused so Jasmin and Stephanie could imagine the very big needle.

Then he exclaimed, "They put the needle right into my bare bottom!"

"Ewwwwwwwww!" screeched Stephanie, Jasmin, and Mum in unison, and everyone rolled about laughing.

What happens when Dad swaps his yellow
BMX bike for his friend's red racer? Find out
in the latest "Words from Daddy's Mouth"—
The Terrible Red Racer.

The story also provides a modern take on
"Murphy's Law." That is, what *can* go wrong,
will go wrong.

www.wordsfromdaddysmouth.com.au

The Terrible
Red Racer

The Terrible Red Racer

By Lily Burgess

Illustrated by Kate Hawthorne

ISBN: 978-0-9922716-2-6 (paperback)
ISBN: 978-0-9922716-1-9 (ebook)

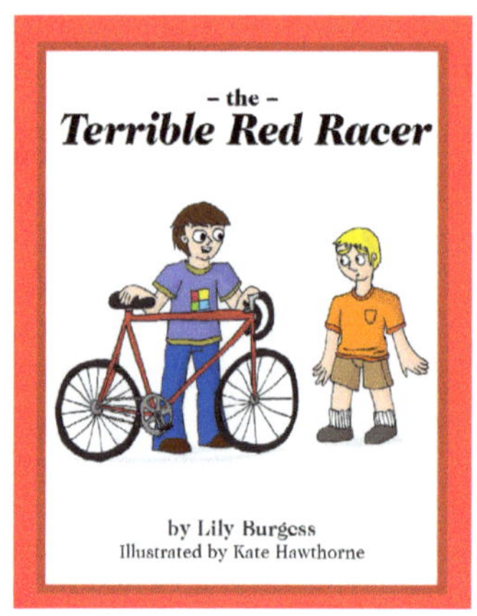

Teachers' Notes

Prepared and written by a teacher with experience in both
whole class and special education.

These notes are made available free of charge for
use in schools.

They may not be reproduced and sold commercially.

The Terrible Red Racer

1 Synopsis

The Terrible Red Racer is the second book in the *Words from Daddy's Mouth* series. In this story, the father recounts how, as a child, he broke his arm when he fell off his friend's bike while riding to soccer practice. He recalls how he was thrown on to the road, and was nearly hit by a car. Although he managed to struggle to the school office to get help, he was turned away. After an agonising wait, his mother arrived on the scene. She took him to the nearest hospital, where he was given a local anaesthetic. However, there was some unexplained delay, and by the time the doctor attempted to re-align the bones in his arm, the anaesthetic had worn off and the procedure was unsuccessful. He was then transferred by ambulance to a second hospital for an operation.

2 Background

While it might seem incredible that so many misfortunes could occur to one child in one day, this story is based on a actual event (with a few embellishments). It took place in the 1980s, in the Australian Capital Territory.

3 Themes

- Reminiscing about childhood experiences
- Overcoming misfortune
- Perseverance

- Learning that life is not always fair and just, and sometimes things go wrong.

4 Writing style

This story is written in the conversational style of a father recounting a child-hood event to his daughters, as told through the voice his daughter, Lily.

The text involves some narration and considerable dialogue. Direct speech is marked by quotation marks (inverted commas). Where there is extended direct speech, continuing over more than one paragraph, the text follows the convention of beginning each paragraph with quotation marks, but only using closing quotation marks at the conclusion of a section of dialogue.

The story also includes an occasional digression, as the father explains concepts and interacts with his daughters.

5 Study notes

To introduce the story:

a. Explain that this is a story a father tells to his daughters, and read the introductory notes.

- Show the students the front cover, read the title, and ask them to predict what a story about a terrible red racer might entail.

- Ask the students if they have ever attempted to ride a bike that is too big for them, and if so what happened.

- Read the story for enjoyment.

Following the reading of the story:

- Discuss the two layers to the story (Dad telling a story to his daughters, and the story about the broken arm). Discuss this with reference to the illustrations on Pages 50 and 51 (*paperback pp. 6 and 7*).

- Identify the main characters in each layer (Dad, his daughters Stephanie, Jasmin and Mum in the first layer, and Dad as a young boy, his friend Jeremy Tobin, the lady driver, the lady in school office, his mum and medical staff in the second layer).

- Ask the students to draw two pictures – one depicting the family listening to Dad telling the story, and the other, showing Dad as a young boy, falling off the red racer.

- Create a story line, showing the events in sequence.

- Identify the digressions. Examples include, early computers (Pages 52–53) (*paperback pp. 8–9*), cassette tapes (Page 54) (*paperback p. 10*), mobile phones (Page 66) (*paperback p. 22*).

- Discuss how the digressions provide context and background to the main story.

6 Activities

- Encourage children to bring examples of 'old' technology to school and set up a display. Items could include early mobile phones, early telephones, cassette players, record players, film cameras, etc. Where possible, date the objects, and ask the students to list their advantages and disadvantages over modern versions.

- The red racer had a special locking device (Pages 56–57) (*paperback pp. 12–13*) that locked unexpectedly (Page 60) (*paperback p. 16*). This

innovation proved a useless and dangerous invention. Have the students
suggest/research other useless/dangerous inventions (examples range from a
rotating icecream cone, to the segway, to hydrogen blimps). Make a list of
these inventions, and have the students debate the pros and cons of each.

- Discuss how the decision to swap bikes led to a series of disastrous events.

- Discuss the reaction of the lady driving the car (Pages 62–65) (*paperback pp. 18–21*). Was she in shock?

- Discuss the reaction of the receptionist at the school (Pages 65–68) (*paperback pp. 21–24*).

- Discuss the consequences of delaying the reduction (realigning the bones in the arm) until after the local anaesthetic had worn off (Pages 72–73) (*paperback pp. 8–9*).

7 Drama

Role-play the decision to swap bikes, the reactions of the lady driver and
the school receptionist, and the delay at the hospital, and have the
students suggest alternative scenarios.

8 Mathematics

- Geometry – discuss / revise triangles. Use rulers and protractors to draw the locking device (Pages 56–57) (*paperback pp. 12–13*).

- Geometry – Discuss / revise right angles (Page 64). (*paperback p. 16*) Use rulers and protractors to draw right-angled triangles.

- Measure 30 cm – the length of the big needle (Page 80) (*paperback p. 20*). Would it have really been this long?

9 Writing

- Students write a recount of a visit they, or a member of their family, made to a hospital.

- Ask the students to imagine what it would be like to break their writing arm. Brain storm what school activities they could and couldn't participate in. Could they do more than just play computer games? (Page 52) (*paperback p. 7*). List the suggestions.

10 Health

- Discuss healthy food, and in particular foods that are rich in calcium, and promote strong bone growth.

11 Social Science

- As this story refers to several generations, this could provide starting point for a discussion of family trees, and the connections between different generations. For example, on Pages 68–69 (*paperback pp. 24–26*), Dad attempts to explain to his daughters that his mum is their gran. Children could be invited to bring family photos to school, and explain the different generations to the class.

12 Science

- In this story, the father tells how he fell off a bike while going down a hill, and the locking device malfunctioned as he attempted to turn. This is an ideal starting point for a science lesson that investigates how the angle of an inclined plane affects the speed of toy cars released from the top of the plane. The experiment can then be extended to discover what happens when an obstacle is placed at the bottom of the inclined plane, and the toy cars are forced to turn.

- As the story also mentions the shoulder bone and forearm bones, the nature of the human skeleton could be investigated.

13 Music

- Learn 'Dem dry bones' song.

14 Worksheets

- Comprehension
- Word Study
- Crossword
- Word Search

The Terrible Red Racer

Comprehension Sheet

Who is listening to Dad's story telling?

____

Who was Jeremy Tobin?

____

Describe a 'Commodore 64'.

____

____

Why do you think Jeremy wanted to ride the yellow BMX bike, rather than his new red racer?

____

____

____

What would you do if you won a prize of $1000 on a radio competition?

1

2

Which route would you choose? Explain why.

Why do you think the lady driver screamed and yelled?

Why do you think the lady in the school office refused to allow a phone call?

Draw four pictures to show what happened when they got to the first hospital

If your arm was broken, would you go to the first or the second hospital?

____

Why?

____

____

____

Do you think Dad exaggerated when he described the last needle as being thirty centimetres long?

____

Why?

____

____

Imagine you are going to visit a friend who has just broken his or her writing arm. You want to take a small gift. Look at the list below and decide whether or not each idea is suitable. Give reasons for your answer.

Gift suggestion	Is this gift a good idea? Yes or No	Reasons
Bunch of flowers		
Pack of cards		
Box of chocolates		
Bag of grapes		
Colouring in book		
My suggestion		

Pretend you are the lady driver. Give your version of what happened.

The Terrible Red Racer

Word study. Write down meanings for these words.

explain
____

popular
____

approach
____

chopstick
____

dislocate
____

mobile
____

plead
____

Read these words:

break	brake

Write a sentence for each:

____

____

Now complete this table

Read	Sound	Write word	Draw a picture
brake	br-ake		
stake	st-ake		
make	m-ake		
fake	f-ake		
lake	l-ake		

cake	c-ake		
quake	qu-ake		
take	t-ake		
wake	w-ake		
break	br-eak		
steak	st-eak		

Word building – read and write these words:

race	racer	races	raced	racing

What happens to the **e** when you add **-ing** to **race?**

Draw pictures for these words:

ambulance		red racing bike	
forearm		yellow BMX bike	
cassette player		zebra crossing	
phone		X-ray	

The Terrible Red Racer

Across

1. The 'Commodore 64' was an early __________.

3. The red racer had a special device that locked the __________.

7. The boy travelled to the second hospital by __________.

8. Early computers had to have games loaded on to them with a __________ tape.

11. How many centimetres long was the very big needle?

12. What was the colour of the BMX bike?

Down

2. How many red buttons did the triangular locking device have?

4. The lady in the car slammed on her __________.

5. The receptionist at the school wouldn't allow a phone call because it was a __________ free day.

6. __________ Tobin owned the red racing bike.

9. The boys were on their way to a __________ practice.

10. Jeremy was given the red racing bike for his __________.

The Terrible Red Racer

```
l  a  m  b  u  l  a  n  c  e  t  b  s  j
e  s  m  a  r  t  p  h  o  n  e  o  j  c
t  r  i  a  n  g  u  l  a  r  r  n  t  o
c  r  o  s  s  i  n  g  n  m  r  e  n  m
r  k  c  a  s  s  e  t  t  e  i  s  t  p
g  a  t  u  n  n  e  l  s  h  b  a  r  u
d  o  c  t  o  r  d  c  c  e  l  r  e  t
c  s  k  e  b  z  l  f  h  s  e  m  a  e
n  c  n  x  r  r  e  s  o  l  b  o  t  r
e  n  w  j  q  f  a  z  o  e  r  n  m  e
t  b  r  o  k  e  n  k  l  e  e  u  e  w
s  o  c  c  e  r  l  x  e  p  a  m  n  a
h  a  n  d  l  e  b  a  r  s  k  b  t  q
c  a  q  p  h  h  o  s  p  i  t  a  l  y
```

ambulance	arm	bones	brakes	break
broken	cassette	computer	crossing	doctor
handlebars	hospital	needle	numb	racer
school	sleep	smartphone	soccer	terrible
treatment	triangular	tunnel		

words from
Daddy's mouth

– the –
Weekend Cash Call

by Lily Burgess
Illustrated by Kate Hawthorne

The Weekend Cash Call

This is a work of fiction. Any similarity to persons living or dead is merely coincidental.

This book is licensed for your personal use only. If in electronic format, a separate copy of this book should be purchased for each person for whom this book is shared. Neither the author nor publisher assumes a duty of care in connection with this book. Some or all of the material in this book may be fictional and for legal purposes you should treat this book as entertainment only and not for instruction.

ISBN: 978-0-9922716-4-0 (paperback)

ISBN: 978-0-9922716-5-7 (Kindle)

ISBN: 978-0-9924210-2-1 (Smashwords)

www.wordsfromdaddysmouth.com.au

Published by D & M Fancy Pastry Pty Ltd

Book Three

The Weekend Cash Call

By Lily Burgess

"Do you know how I used to make money when I was growing up in the 1980s?" asked Dad.

"You used to mow lawns," stated Stephanie, remembering Dad's stories.

"Yes," said Dad. "The other thing was to try to win things from the radio, so I would still get new things without having to work as much."

"Radios are so old school," sighed Stephanie.

"When I was growing up in the 1980s, we didn't have iPods or music streaming or even CDs. Some people had record players, which were really big boxes that you put pieces of black plastic about the size of a dinner plate on and then they spun around to play music.

"Other people had cassettes which were about the size of an iPhone and had two holes in the middle that allowed for spinning wheels to sit inside them. Those wheels spun around and pulled a piece of tape through the cassette, and the cassette player played music."

"Were cassette tapes what you used when you wanted to play a game on Jeremy Tobin's Commodore 64, Dad?" asked Jasmin, remembering *The Terrible Red Racer* story.

"Yes, that is exactly what we had to use. Our family didn't have a cassette player for many years. We had one record player that your Gramps, my dad, owned. Later we bought a cassette player, but for a very long time we had just one cassette player for the whole family. Eventually I saved up enough money to buy a cassette player that also had a radio with it. It was very modern at the time," Dad said.

"Was that called a Boom Box?" asked Stephanie.

Dad laughed. "This was even before Boom Boxes. The sound quality from my cassette player was terrible compared to speakers nowadays, and even though it also had a radio, often it was impossible to pick up any radio stations. The signal was so poor because I lived in a bit of a ditch and the radio towers needed to be in direct line of sight to get a signal.

"When I was growing up, there were only two radio stations that I could listen to. One was run by the government and it only had people talking about current news events."

"Boring," interrupted Stephanie.

"Exactly," said Dad, grinning.

"The cool people listened to the other station called 2CC."

"Were you a cool person, Dad?" asked Jasmin.

"Absolutely," grinned Dad,

"I think that is a matter of personal opinion, Jasmin," said Mum.

Ignoring her, Dad went on. "2CC had shows like the Top 8 at 8, where you could phone in and vote for your favourite song that day and then all the votes got added up and the DJ played the eight highest scoring songs at 8 pm."

"Dad, the radio stations still do that!" added Stephanie.

"There was another DJ who ran a show that was on every Sunday afternoon called 'Take 40 Australia'. This show played the top 40 songs according to the records that had been sold across Australia in the previous week."

"That show is still on too," said Stephanie impatiently.

"That's right," said Dad. "I used to listen to 2CC every morning before I went to school, and then every afternoon as soon as I got home, while I did my homework, until just before I went to bed.

"I used to try to win the competitions that were run on the radio. In fact, around 1983 there was a competition called the 'Weekend Cash Call'. I went within 2 cents of winning. If I had won it, I would never have had to work again," Dad added, grinning.

"The Weekend Cash Call competition was by far the most valuable and exciting competition that I ever tried to win," Dad explained. Mum rolled her eyes.

"What do you mean, Dad? How many competitions did you win?" asked Jasmin.

"Over the years, I must have won about 30 different competitions," stated Dad proudly.

"Wow!" said Avey. "Did you ever win any Barbie dolls?"

Dad laughed, "No, I didn't win any Barbie dolls. The first thing I ever won was a vinyl record by a musician named Bruce Springsteen."

"Is he still around?" said Stephanie.

"Yes, he is still quite famous. At the time I won the record, around 1983, I was about ten and he was not particularly popular. Often with the competitions that I won, it was usually for things that other people didn't want to win.

"To win a competition, you needed to be the first person to call the radio station. I listened to the radio a lot, which meant I was able to work out when a DJ would tell people to phone in. A lot of the DJs would play a song at around 35 minutes past the hour and as soon as that song finished, they would ask people to phone in.

"I would set myself up in the kitchen right next to where the phone was and where Mum or Dad were working. Then I would listen from half past the hour and start dialling the phone over and over again towards the end of the song.

"This was very hard work, because I didn't have an alarm clock or anything to remind me to go and sit in the kitchen. Also, we only had one phone and it was plugged into the wall."

"Plugged into a wall?" quizzed Jasmin, trying to imagine this.

Dad nodded, "Not just plugged into a wall, but the hand set was joined to the phone as well. The phone had a big dial on it. You had to put your finger into a little hole above each number and then spin the dial forward."

Jasmin scrunched her nose again.

"I would try to make the phone work as fast as possible to be the first caller. My world record for dialling the phone number to 2CC was about 12 seconds."

Jasmin's eyes widened.

"That is soooooo slow, so last century," said Stephanie.

"Technology has given you great opportunities that weren't available when Mum and Dad were your age," Mum said.

"Exactly," Dad nodded. "There was no speed dial back in the '80s."

"But my speedy dialling did pay off as I won records by Bruce Springsteen, Mick Jagger, John Farnham and Mondo Rock. I won the exact same record by Bruce Springsteen three times. Another one that I won was by a band named The Cockroaches and they actually became The Wiggles a few years later."

"Wow," screamed Avey.

"Why did they allow you to win so many times, Dad?" asked Jasmin, giggling at the thought of Dad carrying lots of big records.

"Seeing I was really good at winning, my friends asked if I could call up for them."

"Wow Dad, no wonder you thought you were cool," said Jasmin.

"Yes, I was popular," said Dad, while Mum chuckled then added,

"Again, that is your personal opinion Matthew."

"The downside was I had to pick up the records from the radio station which was about a half hour drive from where I lived.

"Another time, when I was in Year Seven – I would have been about 13 years old – I won 15 double passes to a movie premiere and ended up taking my whole class to the movies. The DJ was there on that night, and he said to one of the ushers in the movie theatre, 'Isn't it great that so many of these kids know each other'."

"What was the movie, Dad?" asked Jasmin.

"The movie was called *La Bamba*. It was about some famous musicians from the 1950s, even though we watched it in the 1980s. It was a bit sad."

"The 1950s was old school when my mum and dad – your nanny and poppy – were growing up," Mum explained.

"Exactly," said Dad.

"What else did you win Dad?" Jasmin asked enthusiastically.

"I first met your mum when I was 19 years old and when she came to visit I had won a prize from a radio station. It was a t-shirt, CD and record set by a band named Midnight Oil. The radio station delivered the prize to my house in a big black four-wheel drive vehicle, which was called a 'Black Thunder'.

"Mum's friend was super impressed, but Mum just rolled her eyes and said 'Whatever.' I can still remember how disappointed I was that your mum was so unimpressed."

Mum laughed, "I can see Dad has his own version of these events. It's not what I remember girls. I was just too nervous to say anything."

"At 22 years old, I won nine CDs from a radio competition called 'Beat the Music', Dad continued. That was pretty cool because I got to select the CDs that I wanted to take.

"Then another time – I must have been about 24 – I won a brand new release CD by another olden days band named The Beatles. When I won the competition, the DJ started talking to me on radio about how he had played the CD so loud in his car that the lining in the roof fell out.

"I told the DJ that I wouldn't have that problem in my car, because the lining in the roof of my car had already fallen out."

Mum laughed remembering this. "That car ended up at the wrecking yard."

"The coolest prize I ever won from the radio was during a competition that Coca Cola sponsored. I was 12 years old at the time; I won a Coca Cola t-shirt, 24 cans of Coca Cola and a Coca Cola bottle that was a real telephone. Those Coca Cola phones are now a collector's item on eBay," said Dad. "Unfortunately, I gave mine away. Sorry girls."

"Ahhh," sighed Stephanie, Jasmin and Avey.

"More recently, I won some CDs from the radio. At the time I was winning them you girls were standing right beside me, but you thought that I was just talking to Mum on the telephone.

"When the DJ replayed the interview with me, I turned the radio up really loud, and you ran around the house screaming, 'Mum, Mum, Dad's on the real radio!'"

"Another time, I called the radio just to talk to the DJ. I talked about Nick Cave."

"Who is Nick Cave?" asked Jasmin.

"Nick Cave is one of the world's greatest ever performers and your mum and I have both met him. He's an Australian entertainer who has done many things for the music and arts industries. You could Wikipedia him," said Dad.

"You met him in real life?" asked Jasmin.

"In real life," said Dad in a hushed voice.

"Ooohh," sighed Jasmin.

"What else did you win, Dad?" asked Avey, wanting to get back to the story.

"I regularly won tickets to go and see live concerts," said Dad.

"The Wiggles," yelled Avey excitedly.

"No, sorry Avey, no Wiggles."

"Ahh," Avey moaned.

"Often, I would win tickets just a day or two before the concert was on. I think the radio station was given a whole heap of tickets to give away to make sure that the crowd was as big as possible," Dad added. "When I was about 18 years old, I won tickets to see a band called The Angels."

"Did they play fairy songs?" asked Jasmin.

"Not really," laughed Dad. "They were a very loud, very alternate band. While I thought they were okay, I didn't want to go to the concert, as I had an exam the next day. I decided to drive my car to the concert and arrive about an hour before the show started.

"I thought that the show would be sold out so I could sell the tickets for more than the standard price to someone who was keen to go," Dad explained, his eyes gleaming.

"Unfortunately the show had not sold out and most of the people interested in going looked like they had just walked off a horror movie set. Everyone seemed to be wearing black leather clothes and had crazy hairstyles, big tattoos, earrings and chains. In 1992, dressing like that wasn't common like it is now. The first person I tried to sell the tickets to yelled, 'Get lost, kid. Go find your mummy.' The next few people ignored me.

"By now, there was only 10 minutes to go before the show started. I ended up selling the tickets to a fellow for 50 per cent less than the standard price because I was desperate to just get back in my car and drive home to my mummy," Dad said, laughing with the girls.

"What was the weirdest thing you ever won, Dad?" asked Jasmin.

"The weirdest thing?" said Dad, pausing to think.

"Ahh, the weirdest thing was when I was 15 years old; the competition was called, 'The Spring Clean'.

"I think the radio station must have been running out of money and ideas, because they advertised that their prize cupboard was overflowing and they were putting together huge gift packs for competition winners. They never disclosed what items were in the gift packs, but I decided I wanted to win one anyway, and I did.

"When I got the pack, all of it was in a plastic bag. It was junk. There were coffee mugs with the handles broken off, paper hats that had been water damaged, and white t-shirts that were so old they had started to go yellow."

"Yuck!" screamed Jasmin. "What did you do with all of that?"

"I took it to school and handed it out to some of the kids there."

"Dad, that's not very nice," said Stephanie, crossing her arms.

"Anyway, my disappointment at getting that prize was nothing compared to the day when I was about 8 years old and I lost the 2CC Weekend Cash Call," Dad said, closing his eyes and pausing to remember the call. After several seconds Mum nudged him to continue the story.

"Okay," said Dad. "Where was I again?"

"You were about to explain how the Weekend Cash Call competition worked," said Stephanie, putting Dad back on track.

"Ok. With the Weekend Cash Call competition, the DJ would announce an exact amount of money, for example, $482.25, just before the news each hour. Then some time during the next hour, the DJ would choose a phone number, at random, from the phone book, and phone that number. If the person who answered the phone call could confirm the exact amount, then they won the money.

"If the person didn't know the amount, then the DJ would help them out by telling them the dollar amount, and the person would only have to guess the cents. In other words, they would have a 1 in 100 chance of winning the money. If they got it wrong, then they would get a $2 scratch-it ticket.

"This competition had been running all summer and for the whole summer I had been writing down, every hour, the exact cash call amount. I had also been making sure I was at home at all times during the day in case we were called.

"This had been going on for six weeks and not once did our phone ring. No one I knew had been phoned by the radio station.

"Then one day, at about 3 pm on a Saturday, my mum came in and said, 'Matthew, this radio station is never going to phone you. You have been inside the house all summer. You are to turn the radio off now and go outside and play.' I said to my mum that I just wanted to wait for ten more minutes and get the next cash call amount and write it down, but after that, I would go out to play and I would leave the piece of paper with her in case our house was called.

"Gran looked me in the eyes and said, 'Outside now Matthew. Move it!' So guess what I did?"

"Exactly as your mother told you, Dad?" asked Stephanie.

"Exactly," grinned Dad, looking over at Mum.

'Exactly,' repeated Mum.

"And guess what happened next?" asked Dad.

"What?" asked Jasmin.

"The phone rang. It was the radio station," said Dad.

"Outrageous," screeched Stephanie, while jumping off her seat.

"Totally unbelievable," said Dad.

Mum rolled her eyes again. "Matthew, are you sure about this chain of events?"

"Of course I am. I had gone to play down near Jeremy Tobin's house and your Gran asked the DJ if they would mind holding for a moment.

"Gran put the phone on the bench and ran all the way there to get me. She was puffing when she got to me and said, 'The radio man is on the phone!' I said, 'Oh my goodness!'

Jasmin shrieked with laughter. "Gran's favourite saying!"

"Then we both ran all the way home again. The DJ had to wait at least 10 minutes and close to 15 for us to get back to the phone.

"I was out of breath when I picked up the phone. Then the DJ asked me if I knew the cash call amount.

"I said No, but I had been listening in the last hour."

"The DJ said that because I had been listening, instead of me needing to guess a number somewhere between 1 and 100, he would allow me to just guess an amount in a 10 cent bracket, somewhere between 40 cents and 50 cents.

"He told me the dollar amount was $622.

"It would have taken me about 10 years of mowing lawns to earn that amount. It was more money than I had ever dreamed of having and I had a 1 in 10 chance of winning it.

"I have a copy of the call on a cassette tape if you want to listen."

Everyone screamed, "Yes!"

"Matthew, you'll need to bring the tape and cassette player in to do that," said Mum.

"Yes, and I know exactly where everything is," Dad responded and within a few minutes he had set up the cassette tape and started to play it.

"Lucky that thing still works Dad," said Stephanie.

"Quiet Stephanie, we want to listen," said Jasmin.

DJ: Hi, is this the Burgess household?

Mrs. Burgess: That's right.

DJ: Mrs. Burgess, is it?

Mrs. Burgess: Yes.

DJ: It's Mike Hammon calling with an official 2CC Weekend Cash Call.

Mrs. Burgess: Oh!

DJ: Do you know the amount for this hour and there's a lot of money too.

Mrs Burgess: Um, look, can I get my son?

DJ: Ok, quick. Gone to get the son. May well be we have a winner here. Let's see what happens, huh! Come on son. Just on the sly, the amount is $622.44. Let's see if they get it. The Burgess household in Flynn. Will we have a winner? Hi, who's that?

Matthew: Matthew.

"But Dad", Stephanie interrupted and Dad hit the pause button, "How come you were so quick coming back? I thought you said it took you at least 10 minutes."

"The radio station edited that bit out. Now listen, here's the best part."

DJ: Matthew. Do you know the Cash Call amount for this hour?

Matthew: I wasn't listening. I have the last hour.

DJ: Matthew, you know what, you're going to kill yourself. It's a lot of money.

Matthew: Oh!

DJ: Look, it's $622 and some cents. Now if you can guess the cents, you'll win all that money for yourself and your family. You should have been listening. Look, here we go. I'll tell you. It's $622 and you guess the cents. It's between 40 and . . . because you were listening last hour, between 40 and 50 cents. How much do you think it is?

Matthew: Oh, how much Mum?

DJ: Quick

Matthew: Ahhh

DJ: Between 40 and 50?

Matthew: 4-4-4-42.

DJ: 42? Oooh Matthew, guess what?

Matthew: What?

DJ: It was 44 cents.

Matthew: Ohhh!

DJ: Look, you should have been listening. Listen Matt, what we'll do is we'll send you and your family out an instant lottery ticket. You never know, you could win thousands of bucks with that.

Matthew: Oh thanks.

DJ: Thanks for playing the 2CC Weekend Cash Call.

Matthew: Bye.

"So my chance at retiring at the age of eight was completely lost and I did not even win anything on the $2 scratch-it ticket that came in the post a couple of weeks later.

"What you won't hear is what your Gran said when I told her that I lost by 2 cents, but I bet you can guess though."

"Oh my goodness!" Stephanie, Jasmin and Avey said in unison as they all fell down laughing.

Listen to Dad's podcasts

In this story, there are references to a number of times when Dad won various things from the radio.

On many occasions, Dad would use his cassette recorder to tape his moment of fame and links to these recordings are available via the podcast section of the Words from Daddy's Mouth website.

Please view my website at www.wordsfromdaddysmouth.com.au under the media tab to listen to these recordings.

Find out about some of the things that dad has won from radio competitions in the latest book from the 'Words From Daddy's Mouth' series - 'The Weekend Cash Call'.

The story provides a modern take on the proverb that 'Fortune favours the brave'.

www.wordsfromdaddysmouth.com.au

$14.95

ISBN 978-0-9922716-4-0

The Weekend
Cash Call

The Weekend Cash Call

By Lily Burgess

Illustrated by Kate Hawthorne

ISBN: 978-0-9922716-4-0 (paperback)

ISBN: 978-0-9922716-5-7 (ebook)

Teachers' Notes

Prepared and written by a teacher with experience in both whole class and special education

These notes are made available free of charge for use in schools.

They may not be reproduced and sold commercially.

The Weekend cash call

1 Synopsis

The Weekend Cash Call is the third book in the *Words from Daddy's Mouth* series. In this story, the father tells how, as a young boy (and even as an adult) he won a number of radio show competitions. Some of the prizes he won were quite valuable, while others proved disappointing. However, his biggest disappointment was missing out on a cash call competition, which would have netted him some $622.44 (a fortune for a child in the early 1980s). He missed out because his mother insisted he go out to play, rather than spend extended time sitting by the phone and listening to the radio. As a consolation prize the station sent him a $2 scratch-it ticket, which proved a non-winner. However, a tape recording of the conversation with the radio announcer proved a source of merriment for all the family for many years.

In the course of his recount, the father explains various outdated technologies (such as vinyl records, cassette players and rotary dial telephones) and mentions a number of popular bands, singers and a movie.

2 Background

This story includes a number of anecdotes from the 1980s to the present day. The earlier stories are set in the ACT, the later ones in Brisbane, Queensland.

3 Themes

Reminiscing about childhood experiences:

- Persistence and perseverance will usually be rewarded.

- Sometimes, despite our best endeavours, we must accept misfortune.

4 Writing style

This story is written in the conversational style of a father recounting child-hood events to his daughters Stephanie, Jasmin and (new family member) Avey, as told by his daughter, Lily.

The text involves some narration and considerable dialogue. Direct speech is marked by quotation marks (inverted commas).

5 Study notes

To introduce the story:

- Ask the students if their parents/ grandparents have ever told stories about their childhood.

- Explain that this is a story a father tells to his daughters, and read the introductory notes.

- Show the students the front cover, read the title, and ask them to predict what a story about a cash call might entail.

- Ask the students if they have ever entered a radio station competition, and if so, whether they have ever won a prize.

- Discuss how difficult it is to win such a competition, and how it is necessary to be extremely patient and persistent to win.

- Read the story for enjoyment.

Following the reading of the story:

b Discuss the two layers to the story (Dad telling a stories to his daughters, and the series of anecdotes relating to the various radio competitions).

- Leaf through the book, and identify the illustrations of Dad telling stories to his daughters (pp. 107, 112, 115, 117, 120, 128, 131, 133, 139, 145 and 146) (*paperback pp. 7, 11, 14, 16, 19, 27, 30, 32, 38, 44 and 45*). Are their clothes the same in each picture?

- Now look at p. 25 (*paperback p. 126*). In this picture, the family wear different clothes. Why?

- Leaf through the book again, and identify Dad's anecdotes.

6 Activities

- Draw up a chart, listing the the prizes Dad won, and where possible, his age at the time.

- List the various bands, singers and the movie mentioned in the story.

- Have the students research cassette players, boom boxes, vinyl records and rotary dial telephones.

- Hold a 'Retro Day', and have the students dress in 1980s style clothing (use the illustrations on pp. 9 & 12 (*paperback pp. 110, 113*) for ideas).

- Ask the students how they earn extra pocket. Graph their various money-making ventures.

7 Drama

- Have students play-act the dialogue on pp. 40–42 (*paperback pp. 141–143*). Then change the scenario (for example, someone else answers the phone, the amount is guessed correctly, the phone drops out at the crucial moment etc) and have the students improvise new dialogue.

---

8 Mathematics

a Discuss the concept of inflation, and have the students research what $622.44 would be worth in current terms.

- On p. 33 (*paperback p. 134*) Dad mentions there was a 1 in 100 chance of winning the competition. Introduce the concepts of chance and probability. Use the internet to access chance and probability games and worksheets suitable for the age/ ability levels of your students.

b Timing was a crucial factor in winning radio competitions (pp. 15, 16) (*paperback pp. 116, 117*). Revise/ introduce telling the time. Discuss the differences between analogue and digital clocks/ watches.

- On p. 29 (*paperback p. 130*), Dad mentions percentages. Introduce this concept, and have the students work out 50% of the price of tickets to the movies, concerts etc.

153

⑨ Writing

- Ask the students to write an account (real or imagined) of an occasion when they won (or failed to win) a competition. Did they win a worthwhile prize (or something of little value, such as 'The Spring Clean' prize on pp. 30, 31) (*paperback pp. 131, 132*). Have the students write about their feelings on receiving (or not receiving) the prize.

- Various singers, bands and the movie 'La Bamba' are mentioned in the text. Ask the students to research the stories behind these entertainers, write a synopsis of their findings, and present this to the class.

⑩ Health

- In this story, the mother insists her son go outside to play because he has been sitting inside for an extended time (p. 34) (*paperback p. 135*). Discuss the importance of outdoor exercise, and the need to balance indoor and outdoor activities.

⑪ Social Science

- This story could be used a starting point for a discussion of trends in the mid to late 20th century. Ask the students to identify the various bands/ singers mentioned in the text, and order them according to the eras when they were most popular. Then draw up a chart. For each decade from the 1950s, identify popular bands/ singers, significant historical events, the general economic conditions, block-buster films and fashions. Theorise as to whether there is any connection between these different aspects of society. For example, do fashions tend to be more extreme during periods of prosperity, and more conservative during economic downturns?

- Investigate how bands, such as the Beatles, have played a role reflecting public sentiment during periods of social change. For example, John Lennon's song 'Give Peace a Chance', became a catch-cry of the anti-Vietnam war movement in the 1970s, and his murder in 1980 inspired dissidents in the former Czechoslovakia to create the graffiti splattered wall in Prague, now known as Lennon Wall.

12 Science

- If possible, locate a rotary dial telephone and time the students dialling a given (non-existent) phone number – compare this with dialling the same number on a touch phone.

- Arrange an excursion to a technology museum (such as the Powerhouse Museum in Sydney or the National Film and Sound Archive in Canberra).

- Set up a class exhibition of out-dated household items (vinyl records, rotary dial telephones, cassette tape recorders, early computers, mix-masters, irons, meat-safes…).

13 Music

Choose bands/ singers mentioned in the story that are suited to the age/ interests of your students. (For example, The Wiggles would be a good choice for younger students, while the Beatles might suit older students). Listen to their music and learn some of their songs.

The Weekend Cash Call

Comprehension Sheet

Who is listening to Dad's story telling?

____

What was Dad's record for dialling the phone number for 2CC?

____

How old was Dad when he tried to win the Weekend Cash Call?

____

Explain what you had to do to win the Weekend Cash Call.

____

____

What would you do if you won a prize of $1000 on a radio competition?

____

____

____

Do you agree with Stephanie, that it wasn't very nice to hand out the prizes from 'The Spring Clean', to the kids at school?

____

Why?

____

____

What would you do if you won 15 double passes to the movies?

____

____

Draw what happened when the mother told her son to go outside and play, and he missed the latest amount on the Weekend Cash Call.

The Weekend Cash Call

Word study. Write down meanings for these words.

valuable
____

proud
____

vinyl
____

famous
____

popular
____

record (meaning 1)
____

record (meaning 2)
____

minute (meaning 1)
____

minute (meaning 2)
____

Read these words:

weak	week

Write a sentence for each:

____

____

Now complete this table

Read	Sound	Write word	Draw a picture
week	w-ee-k		
seek	s-ee-k		
feet	f-ee-t		
street	s-t-r-ee-t		

Read these words and write a sentence for each:

sent

____

____

cent

____

____

scent

____

____

Word building – read and write these words

record	records	recorded	recording

Draw pictures for these words:

theatre		vehicle	
tickets		coffee mug	
scratch-it ticket		t-shirt	
record		paper hat	

Explain the proverb: 'Fortune favours the brave':

The Weekend Cash Call

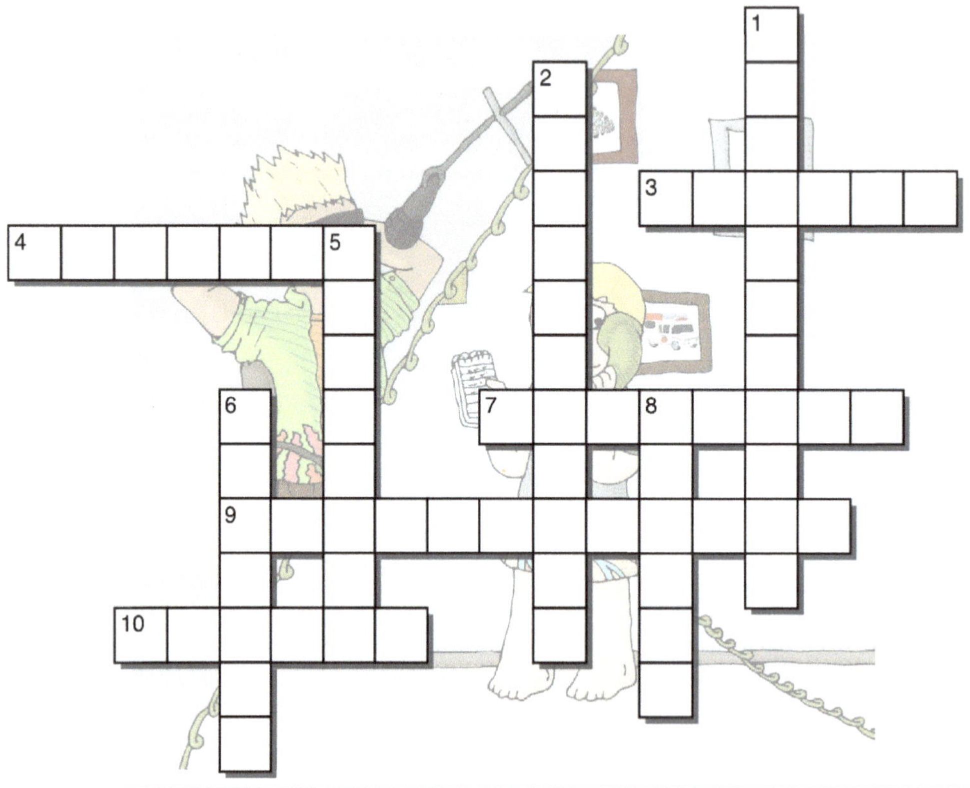

Across

3 Over the years Dad won about _________ on his arm.

4 The DJ had to wait close to _________ minutes before Mum and Matthew got back to the phone.

7 Dad kept a _________ tape recording of the Weekend Cash Call.

9 The four-wheel drive car that delivered the prize to the door was called '_________'

10 The Weekend Cash Call competition had been running all _________

Down

1 The first record Dad won was by a musician called 'Bruce _________'

2 The Wiggles band were once called 'The _________'

5 Who was the performer Dad met?

6 What was the name of the movie Dad took his class to?

8 The 'Take 40 Australia' show was on every _________

The Weekend Cash Call

```
i  c  c  r  c  f  b  h  x  c  l  b  m  x  g
l  l  o  x  q  j  q  c  v  c  c  f  o  t  r
c  w  u  n  s  k  r  r  p  a  o  p  n  e  e
r  a  p  f  c  y  l  e  h  s  m  r  e  c  c
e  b  l  j  d  e  n  d  o  h  p  m  y  h  o
j  u  t  l  o  o  r  i  n  a  e  g  w  n  r
b  t  a  d  l  q  u  t  e  r  t  c  e  o  d
q  m  p  o  l  y  a  c  a  r  i  l  e  l  i
l  g  e  o  a  z  c  z  j  k  t  w  k  o  n
q  p  j  s  r  z  j  f  p  p  i  b  e  g  g
d  i  a  m  i  n  u  t  e  s  o  l  n  y  j
w  r  d  u  a  l  x  h  p  m  n  k  d  k  e
p  e  r  f  o  r  m  e  r  r  a  d  i  o  f
t  i  c  k  e  t  s  w  l  i  s  t  e  n  o
s  f  k  r  e  c  o  r  d  s  f  k  y  s  x
```

call	cash	competition	concert
dollar	listen	minutes	money
performer	phone	radio	recording
records	tape	technology	tickets!
weekend!			

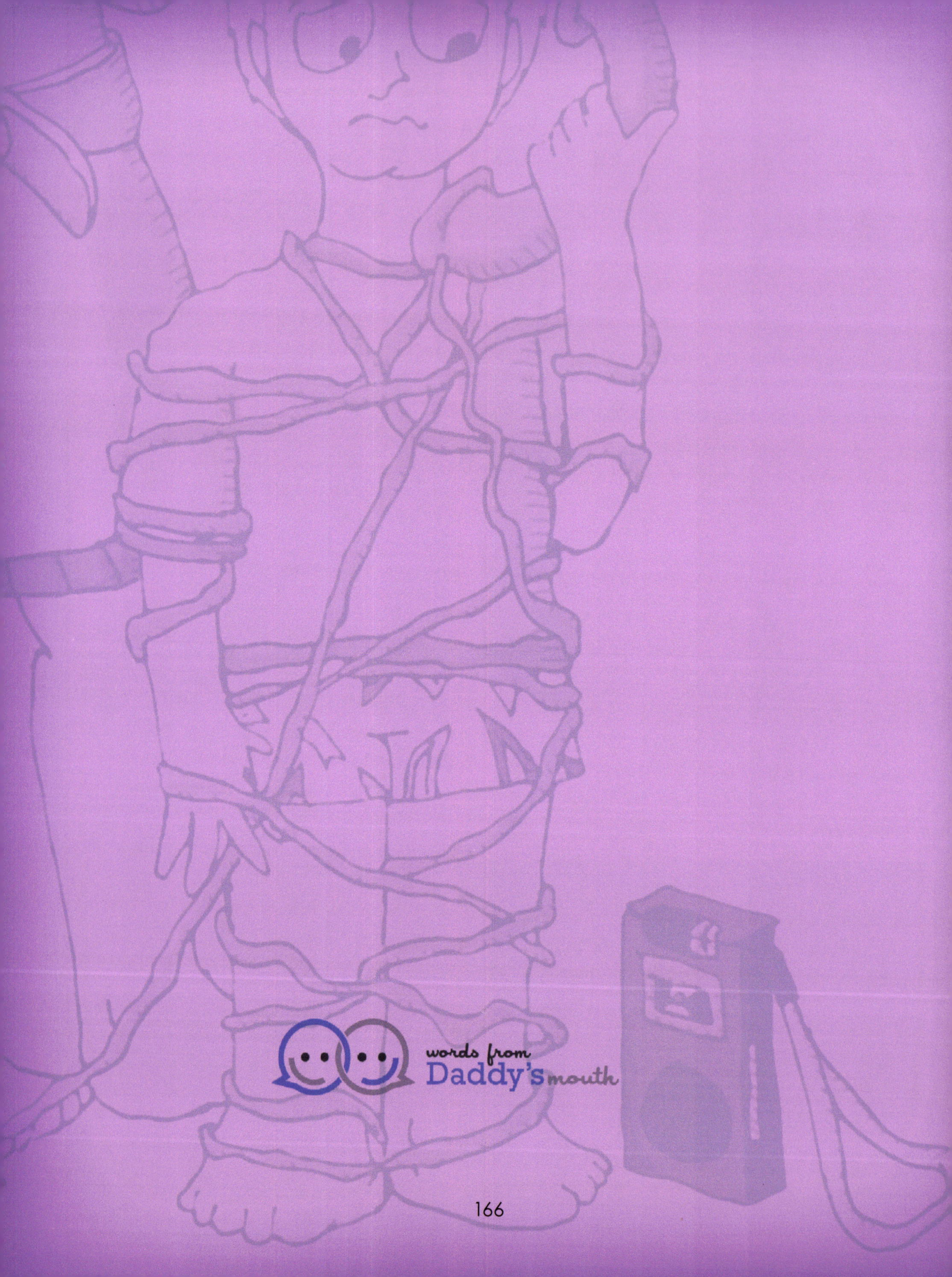
words from
Daddy's mouth

– the –
Brandings Game

by Lily Burgess
Illustrated by Kate Hawthorne

The Brandings Game

This is a work of fiction. Any similarity to persons living or dead is merely coincidental.

This book is licensed for your personal use only. If in electronic format, a separate copy of this book should be purchased for each person for whom this book is shared. Neither the author nor publisher assumes a duty of care in connection with this book. Some or all of the material in this book may be fictional and for legal purposes you should treat this book as entertainment only and not for instruction.

ISBN: 978-0-9922716-6-4 (paperback)
ISBN: 978-0-9922716-7-1 (Kindle)
ISBN: 978-0-9924211-1-3 (Smashwords)

www.wordsfromdaddysmouth.com.au

Published by D & M Fancy Pastry Pty Ltd

Book Four

The Brandings Game

By Lily Burgess

"Remember how I had to repeat Year 6 because I broke both my arms?" asked Dad.

Jaz, Stephanie and Avey all nodded; Jaz and Stephanie because they recalled the story, and Avey because her sisters were nodding.

Dad continued. "After I broke my right arm and the plaster cast had been on for 2 months, it was removed with the biggest pair of scissors I had ever seen."

"How big?" interrupted Avey.

"Almost as big as you Avey," said Dad. Avey giggled.

"Is that true, Matthew?" Mum asked. Dad ignored the question and moved on with his story.

"As soon as the cast was off, I enjoyed getting back into all of the sports and games that I loved playing, like soccer, cricket and running. However, at school, I mostly played handball, British Bulldogs 1,2,3 and Brandings."

"What is British Bulldogs 1,2,3 Dad?" asked Stephanie.

"That was a game where we had our entire class line up on one end of the soccer field, and one person would be nominated to stand in the middle of the field. When the person in the middle called out, 'Go British Bulldogs!', the whole class tried to run to the other end of the ground. The person in the middle would try to tackle people onto the ground and then hold them down and yell out, 'British Bulldogs 1,2,3!'

"Anybody captured then stood in the middle with the original person, so that they could tackle people as well. This process kept going over and over again until eventually there was only one person left trying to run across the field. That person would win if they could get across the field without being caught and tackled by any of the people standing in the middle."

"Wow!" said Jaz.

"That sounds really dangerous!" Stephanie said.

"Yes, really dangerous," said Avey, her eyes wide with concern.

"It was very dangerous," whispered Dad, "but I was so good at it that I never got hurt."

Mum rolled her eyes. "Matthew, is this story appropriate?"

"Mum, you are interrupting the story," said Stephanie.

"Did you break your left arm while you were playing British Bulldogs 1,2,3?" Jaz asked.

"No Jaz," said Dad, "I broke my left arm while playing Brandings."

"What's Bandings Dad?" asked Avey.

Dad laughed. "It was called 'Brandings' Avey, not 'Bandings'. Brandings involved everyone in the class playing a game like hide-and-seek, but with a tennis ball.

When the person with the tennis ball spotted somebody else who was playing the game, then they would throw the tennis ball as hard as they could to try to hit or 'brand' the other person. If they hit the other person, then that person was 'up', which meant they had to run around with the tennis ball and find somebody else to throw it at.

"You had to be a fast runner, an accurate shot and be able to hide well, to be good at Brandings, and luckily, I was excellent at all these things."

Mum coughed and asked, "Are you sure about this Matthew?"

"Then why did you break your left arm Dad?" asked Stephanie.

"Yes Matthew," Mum said.

"I was excellent at Brandings as I said; it was just that I was very bad at jumping over high walls."

"What do you mean?" Jaz asked.

"I will explain more in a moment," Dad continued. "Firstly, do you know why the game was called 'Brandings'?"

All three girls put their hands high up into the air and yelled, "I know!"

"OK then Avey, why do you think the game was called 'Brandings'?" Dad said, smiling at Avey.

"Coz, it was not called 'Bandings'." Everyone laughed.

Jaz then jumped in, "Because that is the name you made up for it, Dad."

Dad grinned. "That's a good reason Jaz, but not the answer."

"I know," interrupted Stephanie. "The reason it was called 'Brandings' was because if you were hit by a tennis ball hard enough, it left a big red mark on you."

"That's right, Stephanie and I can confirm those brands hurt a lot."

"Come on Dad, tell us what happened on the day you broke your arm!" Stephanie moaned impatiently.

"Well," said Dad, "we were playing Brandings during little lunch – you call it first break nowadays – and it was almost time for the bell to ring to go back to class. As I came around one of the classroom buildings, I saw someone with the tennis ball, and guess who it was?"

"Mummy?" asked Avey with a big grin.

"No Avey, Mummy and Daddy had not met yet. The person I saw was the boy who owned the bicycle known as 'The Terrible Red Racer'!"

"Jeremy Tobin!" yelled Jaz and Stephanie in unison.

"Yes, Jeremy Tobin was 'up'. I knew that Jeremy was good at Brandings, but not as good as me," said Dad, puffing up his chest. "So I decided I would need to run as fast as I could while zigzagging. If Jeremy threw the ball at me, I thought I should be able to dodge it. So I decided to run around the side of the classroom and then into a courtyard area. The courtyard had a high wall built all the way around it. There were also some seats next to the far end of the wall."

"How big was the wall?" asked Jaz.

Dad stood up and held his arm about halfway up his body. "About as tall as you Jaz. About 1.2 metres."

"How come?" asked Avey. Everyone laughed at Avey's favourite saying.

"That is not actually very high," said Stephanie.

"It was very high when you consider what I decided to do next," Dad said.

"What did you decide to do?" asked Jaz.

Dad paused, took a big breath, and sounding just like a horseracing announcer, he said, "I raced into the courtyard, then realised that Jeremy Tobin was catching up to me and that I wouldn't be able to get out of the courtyard by going back from where I had come. I decided I would jump up onto one of the chairs, then onto the top of the wall, then down onto the concrete on the other side, and keep running really fast." Dad took another deep breath.

"That does not sound dangerous to me," said Stephanie.

"It probably wasn't too dangerous if I had actually done what I planned to do, but guess what I did instead?" asked Dad, remembering what had happened.

The girls were silent while Dad gathered his thoughts.

Eventually, Mum said, "Matthew, could you please get back on track with the story."

"Oh sorry," said Dad, "Instead of jumping off the wall, I decided to do a dive roll."

"What's a dive roll?" asked Jaz.

"A dive roll," said Dad, as he stood up to demonstrate, "is something like this."

Dad suddenly jumped onto one side of the bed and then rolled over and over and over before falling off the other side with a loud thud and a grunt.

"You OK Dadda?" asked Avey, as the other girls started to giggle.

"No," groaned Dad, "I bumped my head."

Mum looked very concerned but once she realised Dad was OK, she said, "Matthew, be more careful please."

Dad slowly got up, rubbing his head and continued the story. "So I jumped onto the concrete wall and started to do a dive roll, while letting myself fall towards the ground. Jeremy had not thrown the ball at me yet, so about halfway during my fall, I realised I would need to push myself off the ground as fast as possible, so I could start running again to make sure I was not 'branded'. To do this manoeuvre, I put my left arm straight out like this." Dad again stood up and demonstrated by putting his arm out.

"Is anyone going to get injured in this demonstration, Matthew?" laughed Mum.

Ignoring the comment, Dad continued. "As I put my arm out, time seemed to slow down. I remember thinking, Matthew, this was how you had your right arm when you were falling from 'The Terrible Red Racer'. Even though I knew I should move my left arm or I would break it, I couldn't. Before I had a chance to take another breath, I heard ..." Dad paused, then clapped his hands together really loudly and shouted, "SNAP."

Avey jumped with fright and ran to Mum for a hug while Stephanie and Jaz rolled about laughing. Dad continued the story, "I knew as soon as I saw the bone popping up at right angles out of my left arm that I had broken it.

"Fortunately, and most importantly (even though I had broken my arm), Jeremy Tobin had missed 'branding' me, because he had aimed at the spot where I would have been if I had managed to get up and start running again. Instead, I lay like a dying bug on the ground trying to get enough strength to pick up my left arm that had become totally numb and felt as heavy as a thousand million kilograms." Dad lay down, re-enacting a dying bug.

Mum and the girls laughed and Mum said, "Matthew, really, is that necessary?"

"It helps the girls better visualise the scene," said Dad, and continued with his story.

"I didn't want to cry so I clenched my teeth like this." Dad pulled a face that made him look like he was smiling. "As Jeremy ran past me to get the tennis ball, he said, 'Hey, great move Burgo, I completely missed you!'"

"I said, 'Yeah, except I broke my arm doing it.' He laughed, said 'Sure' and ran off. Can you believe it?"

"How come?" Avey asked again, then covered her mouth and giggled.

"How come?" repeated Dad. "I'm not sure Avey, but guess what I decided to do?"

"What?" asked Stephanie.

Dad paused and started daydreaming again.

Seeing how excited the girls were, Mum tried to encourage Dad and said, "Come on! Please finish the story Matthew!"

Dad woke up from his daydream with a jump. "Did you know that Gran was a primary school teacher?"

"Yes," said Jaz, "she now helps me with my reading."

"When I was your age, she was a relief teacher. Relief teachers fill in for other teachers when they are away, which means that the relief teacher could be working at any one of dozens of different schools throughout a town on any particular day."

"We know that Dad, we have relief teachers as well you know," said Stephanie.

"OK, but guess where Gran was being a relief teacher on this particular day?"

"Your school?" asked Jaz with a big grin.

"Yes, at my school. Can you believe it? I decided to go to the teachers' staffroom and find my mum, your Gran. The problem was that I had to walk through two sets of heavy doors. Because I was using my right arm to hold up my left arm, I had to squeeze the top of my right arm into the handle of each door and use my body weight to pull the door back. Then I used my leg to keep it open as I rushed through the door. It was very, very difficult to open each door. It took me a long time to get to the staffroom. When I got there I asked one of the teachers near the door to see if Mrs Burgess was available, and after a period of time, Gran came out to see me. She did not look happy."

"I said, 'Mum, I've broken my arm.' Then guess what your Gran said?"

"That you were a naughty girl?" asked Avey seriously, forgetting that Dad had been a boy at the time.

"No, not quite," laughed Dad, "what Gran said was, 'That's nice darling.' Guess what she did then? She closed the door and walked back into the staffroom. Can you believe it?" Dad said.

"Even worse, the door that Gran closed on me, automatically locked, so I had to kick the door with my foot to try to get someone to open it. It took a long time before another teacher came out. Instead of asking to see my mum, I barged into the staffroom and searched for her. I found her near the back of the room talking and laughing with some other teachers.

"This time I stood right in front of Gran and said, 'Mum, I have REALLY broken my arm. LOOK!' I showed her the bone almost popping out of my skin. Guess what Gran said this time?"

Stephanie and Jaz were totally silent as Avey squeezed Mum tightly.

"This time, she screamed, 'Oh my goodness Matthew, you have broken your arm!'

"Oh my goodness is Gran's favourite saying," laughed Jaz.

"Yes, it is. Gran then got me help straightaway and organised Gramps to drive me to the hospital, so my arm could get fixed. Luckily, unlike with my right arm, everything went pretty well at the hospital."

"You mean you didn't get to go in an ambulance Dad?" asked Stephanie.

"That's right Stephanie, there were no ambulances needed this time. The worst thing that happened this time was that while I was waiting for Dad to pick me up, I was sitting at the front of the classroom. Gran said 'Sorry for not believing you. The way you were clenching your teeth, it looked like a big smile and that you were playing a joke!'"

"What was bad about that?" asked Jaz.

"There was nothing bad about what Gran said, it was what she did." Dad then moved in closer and whispered, "She gave me a big, squishy cuddle and a sloppy kiss in front of my WHOLE class."

"Ewwwwww!" Stephanie, Jaz and Avey screamed as they fell over laughing.

For Dad, there was something even worse than The Terrible Red Racer, and this was "The Brandings Game"—the latest book in the "Words from Daddy's Mouth" series.

The story also provides a modern take on the proverb "Look before you leap".

www.wordsfromdaddysmouth.com.au

Teacher's guide

The Brandings Game

The Brandings Game

By Lily Burgess

Illustrated by Kate Hawthorne

ISBN: 978-0-9922716-6-4 (paperback)

ISBN: 978-0-9922716-7-1 (ebook)

Teachers' Notes

Prepared and written by a teacher with experience in
both whole class and special education

These notes are made available free of charge
for use in schools.

They may not be reproduced and sold commercially.

The Brandings Game

1 Synopsis

The Brandings Game is the fourth book in the *Words from Daddy's Mouth* series. In this story, Dad tells how he broke his left arm. (The story of how he broke his right arm is recorded in *The Terrible Red Racer.*)

This story begins with Dad explaining to his daughters the rules of two playground games – British Bulldogs 1,2,3 and Brandings. He then explains how, when trying to dodge a ball being thrown at him during a game of Brandings, he attempted a dive roll over a courtyard wall. As he landed on his outstretched arm he heard a loud "snap". By coincidence, his mother was working as a relief teacher at his school that day. So, he went to the staffroom to find her. When he told her he had broken his arm (again), she mistook the grimace on his face for a smile and thought he was playing a practical joke. Once she realised he wasn't joking, she arranged for her husband to take him to hospital, where the arm was set in plaster.

The story concludes with Dad recalling his worst humiliation of the day – the hug and kiss his mother gave him – in front of the whole class!

2 Background

This story is set in the ACT during the 1980s.

3 Themes

Reminiscing about childhood experiences:

Considering the consequences of your actions.

4 Writing style

This story is written in the conversational style of a father recounting childhood events to his daughters Stephanie, Jasmin and Avey, as told by another daughter, Lily. The text involves some narration and considerable dialogue. Direct speech is marked by quotation marks (inverted commas).

The story includes the interactions between the father and his daughters as he tells his story. Their different reactions to his statements and questions reflect their interests and levels of understanding.

5 Study notes

To introduce the story:

a Ask the students if their parents/grandparents have ever told stories about their childhood.

- Explain that this is a story a father tells to his daughters, and read the introductory notes.

- Show the students the front cover, read the title, and ask them to guess what a Brandings Game might entail. Do they play a similar game, and is it dangerous?

- Ask the students what they should do if they get hurt in the playground.

- Ask the students about the consequences of playing practical jokes.

- Read the story for enjoyment.

Following the reading of the story:

b Discuss the two layers to the story (Dad telling a story to his daughters, and
the story about the rusty nail). Discuss this with reference to the illustration
on Page 14 (*paperback p. 179*).

- Identify the main characters in each layer (Dad, his daughters Stephanie,
Jaz and Mum in the first layer, and Dad as a young boy, his school friends
and teachers in the second layer).

- Ask the students to draw two pictures – one depicting the family listening
to Dad telling the story, and the other, showing Dad as a young boy,
injuring himself on a rusty nail.

- Create a story line for the rusty nail story.

- Identify the digressions (early computers, responsibilities in the final year
of Primary school, sports and games, the rusty car floor…).

- Discuss how the digressions help to provide context and background to
the main story.

6 Activities

- Draw up a set of alternative rules for British Bulldogs 1,2,3 and Brandings,
so they can be played more safely.

- Have the students make a model of the classroom and courtyard as Dad
describes them.

7 Drama

- Have the students re-enact the story – retelling the majors events in their own words.

- Make puppets for each of the main characters, and turn the story into a puppet show.

8 Mathematics

- On p. 17 (*paperback p. 182*) Dad explains the courtyard wall was about 1.2 metres high. Measure this distance on the ground, and have the students attempt to long-jump it.

- On p. 22 (*paperback p. 187*) Dad says his arm was as heavy as "a thousand million kilograms". Work out how many zeros in a thousand million.

- Obtain some scales, and weigh various objects in the classroom, noting those that weigh around one kilogram.

9 Writing

- Have the students list the rules for British Bulldogs 1,2,3 and The Brandings Game.

- Have the students invent a new playground game, and describe how it should be played.

10 Health

- Arrange for a nurse to visit the school and talk about basic first aid, and how to deal with an emergency such as a broken arm.

- Ask someone who has recently suffered a fracture to talk to the students about their experiences.

- Ask the students to bring any X-rays they may have at home of fractures limbs. Set up a display.

- Discuss the importance of eating a balanced diet, and especially calcium-rich foods to ensure strong bone growth.

11 Social Science

British Bulldogs 1,2,3 and The Brandings Game both had a set of rules. Discuss the need for rules in a society. Draw up a set of rules for day-to-day classroom management, behaviour on excursions, computer use… etc. Display these rules in a prominent place.

 # Science

- For older students, it may be possible to obtain a model skeleton and use this to name the various bones. Younger students might prefer models of dinosaur skeletons.

- Compare the human skeleton to the skeletons of other mammals.

---

13 Music

- As a follow-up to *The Terrible Red Racer*, it was suggested the students learn 'Dem dry bones' song. Revise this song.

---

14 Worksheets

- Comprehension
- Word Study
- Crossword
- Word Search

206

The Brandings Game

Comprehension Sheet

Who is listening to Dad's story telling?

____

Which arm did Dad break in this story?

____

List six sports and games Dad enjoyed playing.

____

Explain how Dad broke his arm.

____

What would you do if you were playing The Brandings Game, and you were trapped in a courtyard?

____

Do you think it was a good idea for Dad to demonstrate a dive roll?

____

Why?

____

Why do you think Avey giggled after she asked, "How come", for the second time?

____

Draw four things that happened to Dad after he broke his arm.

The Brandings Game

Word study. Write down meanings for these words.

daydream

automatic

dangerous

squeeze

ignore

consider

continue

interrupt

| sure | shore |

Write a sentence for each:

____

____

Explain the proverb: 'Look before you leap':

____

____

____

Now complete these tables:

Read	Sound	Write word	Draw a picture
broke	br-oke		
woke	w-oke		
spoke	sp-oke		
bloke	bl-oke		

In this story Dad uses similes, when he says:

"as heavy as a thousand million kilograms" and "I lay like a dying bug'.

Complete these similes:

The car was as slow as

The grass was as high as

The tree was as tall as

The boy was as quiet as

The stars twinkled like

The night was as dark as

The air was as cool as

The river was as wide as

The Brandings Game

Across

3 After he broke his arm, Dad had a
_________ cast put on his arm

7 Giant _________ were used to cut off the
plaster.

9 This time, Dad did not need to go to
hospital in an _________ .

11 Dad was not very good at _________ over
walls.

12 Dad's mum said, "Oh my _________ ".

Down

1 When he was little, Dad used to play
British _________ 1,2,3.

2 Dad played brandings with a _________ .

Dad had to go to _________ when he
broke his arm.

5 Dad ran into a _________ .

6 When Dad broke his arm, it felt as a heavy
as a thousand million _________ .

8 Dad's mum was a relief _________ .

10 When he broke his arm, dad fell down like
a dying _________ .

The Brandings Game

```
x  p  l  a  s  t  e  r  q  x  p  v  b  a  l
q  s  e  r  y  h  t  k  l  m  n  o  d  n  a
y  h  t  z  i  g  z  a  g  d  c  p  a  n  u
a  m  c  o  q  g  y  m  y  a  o  e  n  o  g
p  i  s  u  r  e  k  d  d  y  u  n  g  u  h
s  e  b  s  q  y  r  j  m  d  r  r  e  n  c
w  f  r  r  d  x  u  r  h  r  t  d  r  c  l
j  v  w  s  o  g  n  b  u  e  y  f  o  e  p
f  m  p  u  o  k  n  m  l  a  a  e  u  j  o
i  r  l  x  o  n  e  o  j  m  r  n  s  v  b
t  e  n  n  i  s  r  g  g  q  d  z  w  o  r
b  r  a  n  d  i  n  g  s  e  i  g  s  i  e
a  h  s  c  i  s  s  o  r  s  r  m  z  b  a
n  q  h  j  c  m  v  t  a  c  k  l  e  c  k
l  h  o  s  p  i  t  a  l  e  j  u  m  p  r
```

announce	brandings	break	broke
courtyard	dangerous	daydream	hospital
jump	laugh	person	plaster
runner	scissors	story	tackle
tennis	zigzag		

ACKNOWLEDGEMENTS

This book is the result of contributions from a number of people, each of whom Lily and Matthew offer deep thanks.

In particular:

1. 'The Burgo Babes' – Stephanie, Jasmin and Aven – the co-stars of the stories;

2. Dyan Burgess (aka Super Mum/Super Wife) – the designer of the beautiful outcomes;

3. Christine Burgess (aka Gran) – the fountain of all knowledge BG (before-Google) and author of all the fun stuff in this book (eg games, teacher notes, activities etc);

4. Carolyn Summers (aka one of the favourite Aunties) – for the fantastic guidance on curriculum referencing; and

5. the team from all corners of the world involved in making the original four books, and now this Complete Guide, a reality.

IDEAS FOR ENGAGING RELUCTANT READERS

Although intended primarily as a stories for individual and whole class enjoyment, these texts have considerable potential as a resource for assisting reluctant readers.

While the appearance of the books suggests a 'chapter book', the reading level required to decode the text is within the range of an average nine year old. Books, such as *The Big Rusty Nail* therefore provide an older child, who is struggling with age-appropriate texts an opportunity to read a more 'grown-up' looking book, without having to deal with words and concepts that that are either too difficult or outside his/her experience. The uncomplicated, almost cartoon like illustrations help to provide contextual information and break the text into user-friendly chunks.

In order to ensure that when a reluctant reader first sees the text, he/she is familiar with as many words as possible, it is suggested that before presenting the actual book, the students complete the **Word Search**. Mastering the Word Search should be a lesson in itself, with the teacher introducing and discussing each word in turn, giving the students strategies to decode (i.e. at this stage, phonically regular words can be sounded or broken into syllables, but non-regular words should be presented as a whole, or the students given some fun way of remembering the word (they can often make their own suggestions). This is also a good opportunity to do a word study (for example, look at the word 'nail', discuss the 'ail' sound, and then find other words with the same sound – sail, rail, pail …. etc. Once the students are really familiar with the words, he/she can then complete the Word Search. It is recommended that the the teacher checks that each student can read every word fluently and without hesitation.

If, after completing the Word Search the students are still struggling with word recognition, introduce other preliminary activities. For example, transcribing a sentence from the text onto a strip of cardboard, then cutting it up into individual words, which the students re-arrange and read, followed by discussing any changes in meaning, can prove an effective learning experience.

Another activity, invariably popular with reluctant readers, is to provide each student with a photocopy of one page of the text. The teacher then reads this page to the students, but deliberately makes mistakes, which the students have to correct. This activity requires some preplanning for the teacher, as the mistakes should encourage the students to use graphophonic (letters and sounds), syntactic (grammatical) and semantic (meaning) cues to identify errors. Even the most disengaged students are usually happy to participate in an activity that involves correcting the teacher!

Once the students are familiar with most of the vocabulary, they can be given the actual books, and encouraged to read the text. However, if the teacher feels the text is still too difficult for students to read readily, it an alternative strategy would be for the teacher to read the text to the students, while they follow the words. The text can then be read aloud together, and finally, when the students are more confident, they can read it independently. During this phase, it is important to focus meaning. It is therefore recommended that teachers encourage students to use context and meaning cues to identify unfamiliar words, and avoid sounding strategies. Listening to a recording of the story while following the text provides another means of encouraging familiarity with the words, while focussing on meaning.

The students can then complete the **Comprehension** and **Crossword** sheets. However, with reluctant readers, these sheets are often best done as small group activities, involving teacher directed discussion, and teacher assisted recording. This should not be seen as 'giving students the answers', but rather as providing the scaffolding necessary to give students the confidence to eventually work independently.

OTHER RESOURCES

Other reading and resources we like to use are listed below.

Some of our favourite books and authors:

- Alice's Adventures in Wonderland – Lewis Carroll
- Animalia – Graeme Base
- Bad habits – Babette Cole
- Diary of a Wombat – Jackie French
- Danielle the Daisy Fairy – Daisy Meadows
- Edwina the Emu – Sheens Knowles
- Fox and Fine Feathers – Narelle Oliver
- Judy Moody Gets Famous! – Mega McDonald
- The Dot – Peter Reynolds
- Where's Wally –Martin Handford
- Winnie the Pooh – A A Milne

Our favourite websites to visit:

Dr Suess's Suessville – http://www.seussville.com/

Peter & Paul Reynolds – http://www.peterhreynolds.com/ and http://www.fablevision.com/

Of course, we spend a lot of time buying books on Amazon and Fishpond.

CURRICULUM RESOURCES

While writing these books and compiling the teacher's/parent's notes and activities we aligned our processes and thoughts to support the current Australian Curriculum. Some of the references we utilised, within the Year 3 and 4 band are below:

ACELT1575 – Recognise that texts are created by authors who tell stories and share experiences that may be similar or different to students' own experiences

ACELY1646 – Listen to and respond orally to texts and to the communication of others in informal and structured classroom situations

ACELA1428 – Explore how language is used differently at home and school depending on the relationships between people

ACELA1430 – Understand that texts can take many forms, can be very short (for example an exit sign) or quite long (for example an information book or a film) and that stories and informative texts have different purposes

ACELT1580 – Retell familiar literary texts through performance, use of illustrations and images

ACELT1577 – Respond to texts, identifying favourite stories, authors and illustrators

ACMMG008 – Connect days of the week to familiar events and actions

ACMNA001 – Establish understanding of the language and processes of counting by naming numbers in sequences, initially to and from 20, moving from any starting point

ACMSP069 – Collect data, organise into categories and create displays using lists, tables, picture graphs and simple column graphs, with and without the use of digital technologies

ACMSP067 – Conduct chance experiments, identify and describe possible outcomes and recognise variation in results

ACADRM031 – Explore ideas and narrative structures through roles and situations and use empathy in their own improvisations and devised drama

ACADRM032 – Use voice, body, movement and language to sustain role and relationships and create dramatic action with a sense of time and place

ACAMUM084 – Develop aural skills by exploring, imitating and recognising elements of music including dynamics, pitch and rhythm patterns

ACAVAM111 – Use materials, techniques and processes to explore visual conventions when making artworks

ACAVAM112 – Present artworks and describe how they have used visual conventions to represent their ideas

References are current as at date of publication from http://www.australiancurriculum.edu.au/